Saving Lenny Franks

By

Ralph Strangis

UNSTABLE PUBLISHING

"You know he got the cure
But then he went astray
He used to stay awake
To drive the dreams he had away.
He wanted to believe
In the hands of love."

-      *Paul David Hewson*

Chapter 1

This is the story of how Lenny Franks almost saved the human race on earth.

He didn't because it was too big a job for any one man and things were already too mucked up when he got into it. But he gave it a good go. Boy did he ever, Lenny Franks and his army. It wasn't really an army like you'd think about an army to tell you the truth. You know, like the US Army.

It was all just too late. And what was the old expression?

A dollar short...

Or maybe a hell of a lot more than a dollar to be really honest. A dollar wasn't much.

Of course, the pity of the human race on Earth was that it was really hard when you talked about them to say they gave it a good run. You know like they used to say about things:

"Yeah – but they gave it a good run..."

No. They didn't. Not hardly at all.

To be ABSOLUTELY clear:

The Human Race was a colossal clusterfuck from the get go and it's hard to fathom how they lasted as long as they did.

Lenny Franks gave it a good run.

Lots of bugs and a few of the animals who were still left made it ok. And some fish. And the planet was still spinning. Of course, the planet was still spinning. The planet was one tough son of a bitch. Been through a helluva lot worse than fifty years of plastic bottles, refinery smoke and cow farts.

Lenny Franks would say

"The planet's fine you idiots we're the ones who are fucked. And by the way, wait till you find out what's really going on out here. These fucking cellphones are gonna be the end of us."

And they'd shake their heads and say

"Poor Lenny Franks…"

And that wasn't the only time people used to shake their heads and say

"Poor Lenny Franks…"

It happened a lot.

To be completely fair about it Lenny Franks was not everyone's cup of tea, and let's get that out there right away. He possessed, as most humans did, some really wonderful and engaging qualities. But he could also be an unmitigated pain in the ass, and just flat-out exhausting and infuriating to be around. He was animated and loud and volatile and sometimes he could get pretty rattled when humans didn't respond the way he thought they should, which was several times daily. And for some reason that eluded Lenny, he found himself constantly trying to instruct humans on how to do things the right way. This chronic practice, quite organically, led to Lenny frequently jumping in to save humans in one form or fashion, regardless of whether the humans wanted or needed Lenny's help in the first place. This was difficult on Lenny and excruciating on everyone else.

Lenny Franks also was probably a little crazy.

Ok, full disclosure, (note: hearing the term *full disclosure* really rattled Lenny) he *was* crazy. But, he was smart and he could memorize all kinds of long passages from books and TV and movies. He thought himself clever and resourceful and resilient and he was right. He had to be those things because he was perpetually getting into it up to his ass. And so, *clever and resilient* comes in pretty handy when a guy becomes hopelessly frustrated with his daily observations and interactions with humans. And these qualities can be especially useful when a guy jumps too quickly, and wants to save something or someone who doesn't need or want to be saved. Like when Lenny Franks tried to save the entire human race from extinction, but that's later in the story.

He sure as hell didn't see things like everybody else. Lenny believed that most humans never gave a second thought to all the stories that were in each of their heads that other humans, like their parents or teachers or friends or bosses or textbook authors or the guys on TV or radio, put in there. Here are just a few of the stories Lenny wondered about that had been dumped into people's heads, generation after generation, by people who had had them dumped into their own heads and were simply repeating what they already knew to the next group:

Like how you had to go to school and be in debt and bang your head on the wall like everybody else until you retired or died. Like how you believed in this GOD if you were from one and place and that GOD if you were from another but your GOD was the right one. Like how you were a Minnesota Vikings fan just because you happen to be born in Minnesota. Like how the boss was always right. Like how you're not supposed to bring up things like dying or oral sex in public. Like who you thought discovered America. Like how legal meant good and illegal meant bad. Like how you regarded poor people depending on how and where you grew up. Like how you regarded rich people depending on how or where you grew up.

And he said things that hardly anybody else would say.

Here are some of the things he would say right off the top of his head:

"How come it's no problem to show nipples and say "Fuck" on channel 1802 but not on channel 1604?

"When you get older and get a different job think about if we really should be charging $ 24 dollars for a bag of popcorn and a cup of soda and then feel free to take action on trying to help change that."

"I give the whole species about thirty years maybe."

"Why the hell would anybody wanna give up their one shot at privacy when they're in their car by looking at their damned cellphone?"

"I'm really not everyone's cup of tea that's for sure."

He was one of the very first to notice what the hell was going on and actually give a shit and try and do something, and everybody had to give him that. But only after it was too late of course. And humans being how they are, it ain't all that surprising that nobody gave him that.

And in the *Banglordian* history logs there would be mention of one Lenny Franks, Jr., one of the humans who almost rallied the whole human race on Earth. How about that? These aliens were impressed by any human who did not spend his or her days looking into tiny screens, or working on new ways to screw each other, or blow up somebody because they wanted to save money on gasoline or because somebody else believed in a different GOD.

There was even discussion among the remaining humans about a statue at the spot at Venice Beach where Lenny Franks and his army were defeated and rounded up. But it was ultimately up to the *Banglordians* and they never heard of statues before.

It was always something. Lenny Franks used to say that a lot too.

"It's always something."

The story of how Lenny Franks almost saved the human race on Earth kind of started with the eclipse. Good lord what a week that was.

Lenny had good jobs but at that moment he didn't have one. He had good friends and at that moment he didn't have so many. Lately he had had a run of bad luck like you read about. Every piece of mail cost him more money and almost gave him a heart attack. He never really understood money anyway but we'll get to that. Every gas station that week was out of gas and that was the truth. The sadder part is that Lenny didn't have any place to go anyway and he had a flat tire.

He had a girlfriend and he loved her a lot and she loved him a lot and they each would tell each other that about fifty times a day. She used to say to him

"Oh, Lenny you're my cup of tea!"

And he would always feel like the happiest man in the world when she did.

She said these things to him even on the day she broke up with him. Lenny cried for days. And he wondered all the time after she broke up with him if he was or ever would again be anybody's cup of tea.

Teddy helped.

Teddy was his Teddy Bear and had been there from the very beginning. His mom or his grandma gave it to him when he was a tiny baby human. He never really got the story right though. If you asked Lenny Franks about Teddy he'd say

"Teddy was about the best friend a guy could have."

and he'd mean it.

And if Teddy could talk about Lenny Franks well you'd be there for days, so thank GOD about the fact that Teddy couldn't actually talk.

One night while Lenny was really sad because of all the regular stuff and now the eclipse and him getting broken up with he and Teddy watched the old movie *Castaway* together. It was one of Teddy's favorites because of Wilson. At the end when Chuck Nolan talked to his friend and said

"So now I know what I gotta do. I gotta keep breathing because tomorrow the sun will rise and who knows what the tide could bring."

That made Lenny feel a teeny tiny bit better. Maybe the tide would bring something in besides hurricanes and whale shit and plastic bottles and toxic chemicals. That got him up and moving.

The whole thing really started years and years before that when Lenny was in Los Angeles and saw things in his brain during what he called the war when he was doing a lot of drugs. It wasn't a war like you'd think about a war though. You know, like the Viet Nam war. Then he started noticing things that really bothered him. He mostly noticed and thought about these things when he was driving and listening to loud music in the car. Little things at first and then bigger things. Here are some of things he noticed and thought about that drove him crazy:

11

How everything was changing so fast and for the worse. How nobody seemed to wanna use their turn signal or even care that it was your turn to merge. How confusing it could be just to buy peanut butter. How you only could go fishing three days a year. How you always seemed to owe more than you had no matter how hard you worked and how much you had. How not being good with money was the worst thing you could be. How you thought you were successful and popular by counting how many checkmarks you got on pictures of food you'd send out there to the world from your cellphone. How that was called sharing. How humans couldn't stop playing cartoon games on their cellphones. How humans didn't read as much and didn't know much. How you had people you called friends just because you clicked on their name on a screen. How humans were looking into these little screens and giving people they didn't even know checkmarks. How you had to be either democrat or republican and how you had to think the other side was ridiculous. How humans would spend all day spinning through mindless gibberish while everything was going to shit.

It was like everybody turned into that Roman emperor who played his violin while the whole damned thing was burning down around him is what Lenny thought was happening.

And so, these things pecked and pecked away at him. The more he noticed things about humans on Earth the louder the pecking got. Then the eclipse and his girlfriend breaking up with him, well, those were the last two straws right there. He couldn't stand it in that little apartment in Texas anymore. he had to keep breathing and get moving. Go someplace. Try. Go find the tide and see what it could bring. *Give it good run.*

He had this feeling about getting back to Venice Beach which is in California, because it's like it was forty years ago for a lot of those people there. Forty years ago, everybody and even Lenny had it way better. The ocean was at Venice Beach, and so was the tide, and who knew what that could bring. The sky was so bright blue there. The sun was friendly, and not like the miserable prick it was all the time in Texas. Lenny had this feeling about if he could get back there and see the ocean, and be under the friendly sun, and be around those humans maybe something would come to him. Somebody had to try and nobody else was trying for him.

So, the whole thing fell to Lenny Franks and nobody else and by God and by Christ he was gonna give it a good run.

Chapter 2

It really was happening and it wasn't just a dream in Lenny's brain during the war. --
---0--------------------

"Large blue planet with salt water and sunlight and oxygen and many caves and tunnels and sticks and plenty of rubber and plastic STOP *Inhabited by young species of morons who won't last long anyway but why chance it* STOP *Estimate with usual tech acceleration entire planet will be empty in .00078 fledgers* STOP *The idiots will probably create some big holes and the air will have radioactive gas but no problem for us* STOP. *Animals and sea life who survive no threat to us* STOP."

- Rufus622, Commander, BL-001 communiqué to Banglordian High Counsel after third grid sweep. (Earth Calendar, February 27, 1961)

* Note - .00078 fledgers are approximately 60 Earth years. (Translation and math conversion by *Katie0429, BSmithsonian Chief Cartographer, Earth Calendar October 22, 2024)*

Chapter 3

BOOM! PUK-OOOSH! WHOKSH! FITSHSHSHSHSH...

This is sorta near the end of the story but it's a good place to talk about now and sometimes in books you jump around a little.

Lenny made it to Venice Beach and he even was talking to his old girlfriend and we'll get to that, but this is the part where his Ciera car caught on fire. He loved Oldsmobiles, and he had this one forever, but now he watched as the flames shot these huge invisible heat shards at the raggedy group of spectators dotting the parking lot at Venice Beach. About all Lenny Franks and Patch could do was watch with the crowd as the few remaining items of Lenny's life were incinerated. Patch was Lenny's new best friend and that's a good story too and you'll find out all about Patch later.

Lenny had no idea if he was losing anything of actual value in the blaze. How can you know what items you'll need to try and save the human race on Earth after all? Or what that whole thing is gonna look like? He certainly didn't know at that moment that the guy wearing the shit-stained blue T-shirt and wearing roller skates holding a banjo standing a few feet away would become one of his most trusted and capable soldiers. But not a soldier the way you'd think of a soldier. You know, like a Marine.

Oh, the fire show was spectacular that's for sure. The tendrils climbed toward the night sky. They were dancing. Brilliant red and orange and yellow and even bright green dancers dancing. Their arms were reaching for something. Something. Yes – something. Hard to say what.

In a tiny corner of his brain Lenny was figuring that the colorful mélange came from a mixture of whatever it was that made up the velour interior of the car, and the paint and glue that Patch had in the plastic bag. If you asked him about it later he'd say that he'd never forget how the whole thing smelled even though he could never describe it.

In a bigger part of his brain is where he was chewing on how pissed off he was at Patch for lighting the Ciera on fire in the first place. And after all Lenny did for him. He basically saved Patch's life is what he did. He found him on the Las Vegas strip and took him to Venice Beach with him. Lenny paid for all the food and the gas and even gave Patch a shower at the Car Wash. Whenever he told the story though, he'd leave out the part about how they met which was Lenny running Patch over on Las Vegas Boulevard.

But because of some of the realizations he discovered on the trip, this was one of those moments where he could recognize the real problem. The real problem was, in fact, Lenny Franks. Why was he always jumping in and saving people? And why was he always mad at people for how they were and for not wanting to be saved or appreciating him saving them? He always paid for the food and gas as long as he can remember, and that's one of the reasons he was bad with money. He had already figured out that maybe he shouldn't get made at people for how they were. He also had severely curtailed his efforts to save people.

The fire was an accident. Lenny would later say that smoking cigarettes on the back bumper with the trunk open wasn't one of his better ideas. Maybe if all the glue and paint weren't in the trunk right next to the blankets and other junk, and if the trunk wasn't open, and if they weren't sitting on the back bumper next to all of it then it would have been ok.

But that's how it was. And so, when Patch flicked the end of his burning cigarette as they started walking toward the beach, and the wind caught it perfectly and blew it right back into the open trunk, well that was that.

The dancing flames were now losing a little fight but the heat they threw off still kept Lenny Franks and Patch several feet away. Except now the homeless humans at the beach were inching in closer. Here's another thing Lenny didn't know about right then. These homeless humans were about the best army a guy could ever want. But not an army like you'd think about an army. You know, like in movies. That's what he'd say later on anyway and that was what probably would have been on the statue. One of them asked if anybody had any marshmallows and the rest of them laughed but not Lenny and Patch or the guy on roller skates with the banjo, who was called Banjo.

"I don't know I don't know I don't know."

Lenny spit out under his breath.

He said to Teddy Bear right after castaway and before the trip started

"Teddy what the fuck. Everybody else has moved on. It's time we moved on. Let's be us. People don't like us well that's on them. We at least be us and try and move on and see what the tide brings maybe we can live with whatever happens."

He wasn't all that confident in what he was saying about all of it but what the hell was a guy gonna do? See, Lenny knew deep in his brain with the images and all that he kept seeing that the human race was living on – what do you call it – when you know you've probably been living – oh yes – *On borrowed time*… That's what the human race had been living on. And although he couldn't see it yet so was he. And for quite a while. When you save people all the time and you act like an asshole and an idiot lots of the time it takes a toll. How they and he for that matter lasted as long as they all did... well

"Christ all FryDEE"

is what Lenny's grandpa would say when things were just unbelievable.

He always kind of knew it. It just got clearer the more he saw. The more he saw humans and how they behaved. The more he looked closer at himself. He wondered if America was worse than other places and he thought so but how could he know for sure.

Damn the world could take pieces out of a guy. And humans could take em out of each other. He figured everybody had had more than enough and for a very long time but they just kept taking it and for a while so did he. They just kept takin pieces out of each other too. Here's some of the ways Lenny noticed how humans kept taking pieces out of each other:

Fees for this and fees for that and exorbitant interest rates and needless protection plans and warranties. $5 dollar coffees where you had to tip the guy. Service charges and delivery charges and then a place for a tip. The guys at the airport take your water then they charge you $4 bucks for a new water. Copays and recurring subscriptions that were impossible to cancel.

Regular people didn't know there was anything they could do about any of it. They believed all the stories that others put in their heads because they didn't know they had any choice. They all looked so fucking tired all the time and so did he for a long time. It was like everybody had all just given, up but didn't even realize they had all just given up. They were fat and tired and miserable. They all had twisted faces and not enough money. They were all staring into their tiny screens all day, even when they were alone in their cars. They couldn't quit or change jobs. They lived to find distractions from their day-to-day lives because their day-to-day lives were largely unbearable. They were stuck. They couldn't even think about how stuck they were, or how lonely they were, or how bad it had all gotten, or they might have poked their own eyes out with coat hangers.

But not Lenny. Not anymore anyways. Deep in his bones he knew the whole thing was coming apart, both with the world and with him. He was gonna get out and get his trim but in no way overly athletic five-foot, ten-inch frame moving even if he was heading off the path. Lenny had this expression he liked to say to Teddy

"Teddy - It's better to be moving in the wrong direction than standing still going forward."

So, Lenny thought it was better that he did something instead of just watching the pieces get hacked away. Lenny Franks wondered if pieces grew back by themselves. He sure hoped so. He would still be mostly bald and everything and he figured that he'd have to keep wearing glasses, but maybe some of the pieces inside could grow back a little. In fact, he thought he could feel some little tiny ones starting to sprout after his time with Patch and every now and then after that, especially when he talked to her. He kind of forgot about that while he watched everything he owned burn up in front of his eyes.

Patch limped up sheepishly to Lenny and said

"Lenny Franks, I sure am sorry about the Ciera. She was a damned fine ride and she brought us a long way together. I ain't gonna tell ya to stop thinkin for just a little while you just do whatever you gotta do. And I swear to God Almighty Himself that I'm gonna help you get your life back if it takes me the rest of my life."

Lenny had so many things he wanted to say to Patch, but the only thing that came out was this tiny grunt you could barely hear. If you looked really close you could see a little vomit on his lower lip.

And as the few remaining dimming dancing flames curtsied and bowed and slinked off the stage escorted by the sand and buckets of seawater from the firemen, Lenny turned and walked away from Patch and shook his head and wondered how many pieces he had left now, and if any of this was worth it or if he ever in his life knew what the hell he was talking about.

Chapter 4

Here's how Lenny's life was before he started on the trip to Venice Beach. Before the eclipse. Way before he met his girlfriend and way, way before she broke up with him, but after he first got the stuff in his head during the war in Los Angeles in the 80's.

Lenny was a salesman. He was actually a damned fine salesman. He had a way with people and boy could he ever talk your ear off. Lotsa times people probably bought the bloody thing just so they wouldn't have to spend any more time with him. He could wear a guy down that was for sure. Ask Lenny's dad, Lenny, Sr. who was always getting worn down by Lenny. But we'll talk about that a few pages from now. Ask his girlfriend. We'll get to that too but you'll have to wait a little longer.

Lenny never did like having a job, and wearing a suit, and justifying himself to other humans who wore suits every day and sometimes even on the weekends. His Uncle Claude used to get so animated and make his eyes big and say

"Lenny, they say there's no slavery any more but they're wrong. There is slavery and it's called jobs. People show up every day for work.

And you don't gotta feed em and you don't gotta house em. And if they don't show up don't worry there's a hundred more waiting to take their place. A *job* Lenny – is the worst thing a guy can have."

Uncle Claude used to cheat at cards but he wasn't wrong about this one, Lenny didn't think. Lenny thought that humans and especially higher ups who wore suits and good clothes every day thought guys like Lenny were a dime a dozen. Hell, these days they thought everybody was a dime a dozen and mostly they were right.

Here's the thing really. Lenny Franks had had quite enough of the world of companies and jobs and meetings and emails with calendar invitations and people sending him pictures with quotes on em and races to get checkmarks on what picture or sentence you sent out there on your tiny screen. Lenny Franks decided he wanted to have very few people he wanted to justify himself to and no emails with calendar invitations. And at the same time, he just got tired of being Lenny Franks. And it's not that he didn't like Lenny Franks.

Oh no, that's not it at all. Being Lenny Franks had lots of advantages and came with a lot of perks. Listen, if you were to ask him about being Lenny Franks he'd say

"The Lenny Franks that everybody knew was good at taking care of me and payin for all the food and gas. And he used to come in handy especially before the war when it came to having orgasms with women."

But there were more important things to think about now and it's hard to think about em if you have a regular job and a boss.

This is the story of his boss at the TV station and it's really a story about most bosses these days. He sure had had his share and most of em were like this one.

His boss at the TV Station where he worked was a man named Clyde Fitzreichal whom everyone called *Riker* and not *Fitz* or *Fitzy*. Apparently Fitzreichal grew up with another boy, one Richard Fitzgerald, who grabbed both *Fitz* and *Fitzy* early on. Fitzreichal launched an unsuccessful campaign to wrest what he believed was his rightful moniker from Fitzgerald.

He never really liked the name *Riker,* but his lobbying efforts were unsuccessful and the name stuck and he made the best of it, but he vowed to never get beat on anything like that again.

Fitzreichal went to a small Eastern University and studied business. After graduation, he married the first girl he fell in love with and together, and with his own Uncle's considerable bankroll behind him they opened a small Laundromat then another then another. LAUNDRA GO-GO grew into the fourth largest Laundromat chain in Rochester, Minnesota before the Fitzreichals sold out to P. Howard Howards, a local entrepreneur who owned several small TV and radio stations.

Howards was so impressed with the young bulldozer that he hired him to be the GM of his flagship TV Station KFGO in Fargo, North Dakota. *Riker* immediately showed a talent for swelling the bottom line through the tried and true practice of fucking everyone with whom he came in contact. He gorged the station's best sponsors. He cut staff indiscriminately while tripling the workload for those whom he allowed to stay.

Then the real magic for *Riker*. Since the remaining employees were all constantly off balance and scared shitless, he got those who stayed to annually accept a smaller salary than they worked for the year before. In private He called this practice FUCT or "Fiscal Usage Compliance Tactics."

Riker then was a bit of a business pioneer and was in the first group of modern American tyrants (after the first celebrity President got the skids greased for em) to redefine how companies would operate and how the world would change.

26

Soon came the start of the unending glory days, where absolutely every working person would be grossly underpaid, inhumanely overworked and usuriously overcharged. Those in the upper one percent club saw they could get away with it and so get away with it, they most certainly did. These higher ups from every industry imaginable colluded with their own governments and each other, and confused and baffled and belittled the weak and the witless and the weary. These captains of industry grinded em all down to the nub. They perfected the language of terms and conditions, and the art of burying the deepest and most devastating cuts inside the tediously tiny and intentionally deceptive and cryptic small print. They schemed to overwhelm the masses with barrages of unsolicited emails and media posts to distract and defraud. They wore down everyone on every side of every transaction. They trickled that shit down on everybody. They got so good at it, and the informational costs for the regular guy to keep up with their shenanigans got so steep, that regular humans eventually just buried their heads a thousand feet into the sand of their tiny cellphones and video screens and watched sports and took lots of prescription pills and drank wine and beer and lined up for more because they had nowhere else to turn.

Later came the second celebrity President, a poster boy for the programs of the first, who rode that hurtling bullet train all the way to the most powerful office in the world. Three decades later while campaigning to get the job for himself and continue to advance the cause, he added his own special spin. It was genius and it was swallowed whole by the poor bastards who believed that they too could become one of the upper one percenters. The truth now was everybody was fucked no matter who was in charge, and the average guy would never become one of them.

The story this guy told was that it wasn't him and his buddies - the guys at the top who were screwing everyone – it was the ones at the very, very, very bottom who were trying to jump ahead of the honest, hard-working real citizens into line.

That seemed like a good enough explanation to them, and so they cheered and screamed and turned out and voted and gave him a shot. It never occurred to them that they had just voted into office one of the very bosses they were all getting screwed by.

Riker and all like him were especially deft at the practice of convincing those under them that their company was perpetually broke, but that they were doing whatever they could for each of them, and that the workers were fortunate to have jobs at all.

Prior to the first celebrity President, and guys like *Riker* and the rest it, was commonplace in America for several decades for a boss to actually reward an employee's loyalty and performance with small annual cost of living raises and bonuses. Even if a company was not always profitable or growing, many bosses and companies, knowing full well that under no circumstance was any worker ever paid remotely what they were worth, and recognizing the value of continuity, would kick a few bucks down not out of any sense of what was right or decent or true – but because they realized that replacing workers might actually cost them more money and time.

Riker believed that everyone needed jobs, and there would be an endless supply of people waiting to take over should any of his employees not want theirs. That logic was hard to argue and it always made Lenny think of his Uncle Claude.

Riker became a sought-after executive and wound up running the same big station that employed Lenny.

So, when Lenny went to *Riker* and said

"I think I'm running out of pieces and I don't really believe all the stories in my head or know who the hell Lenny Franks really is and the way things are with how companies work and how the world works and all the shit in my brain from the war I just don't think I should be here anymore."

Lenny had heard once or twice before that if you jump – don't worry – the net will appear and catch you.

Riker had no fucking idea what Lenny was talking about. But he quickly realized what this might mean to the bottom line so he embraced the idea. He shook Lenny's hand and wished him well. Then he got quickly to the business of replacing Lenny with an even less expensive alternative. He explained to Lenny's replacement immediately that the company was going broke, and that he'd be happy to have him but at a price less than what he was paying Lenny. Lenny's replacement couldn't believe his good fortune.

And on that day on his way out of the office, Lenny Franks jumped. And if you asked him on his way out the door if he was sure about any of it he would say he was sure of just one thing – that there was no way in hell was there going to be any fucking net.

CHAPTER 5

The day after Lenny watched Castaway with Teddy, he decided he had to call Lenny Franks, Sr. and tell him about what he was going to do next, and maybe see if he could ask him for a few bucks. This was the toughest part because, to be truthful about the whole thing, Lenny Franks, Sr., thought his son was a dipshit, and had over the years given him more than a few bucks. With each check came another admonishment to Lenny, Jr. and more little reminders that he was, in fact, a dipshit. To be fair, Lenny had given him ample ammunition over the years to come to that conclusion.

Lenny Franks, Sr. was a very powerful businessman who worked at the firm of *Steigerflazhen, Franks & Steigerflazhen*, and in a different state than where Lenny was. As points of fact, the Steigerflazhens weren't related to each other, and Lenny Franks Sr. was in fact *The Franks* on the letterhead. The firm specialized in things the younger Lenny Franks did not understand nor could ever describe.

Franks, Sr. wore a suit every day and didn't justify himself too much to anybody but, being married for the second time, he hardly ever got to pick the restaurant. He spent most of his time in the company of other guys who were married for the second time and who also hardly ever got to pick the restaurant. He made lots of money but wrote lots of checks, many of them over the years either directly to or on behalf of his namesake.

Yes, the elder Franks exhibited both great pride and overwhelming relief when Lenny got through the war mostly intact, and joined the rest of the population in what the father saw as the most noble pursuit of tirelessly and for all eternity banging ones' own head on a cement wall. He was also genuinely quite proud of Lenny for turning things around and rising in his profession and earning his own way.

However, when it came to the younger Franks' transgressions, Lenny Franks, Sr. possessed the memory of an elephant, and in case that should ever fail, he kept a makeshift ledger on a file folder at the ready in the top desk drawer of his office listing every mistake Franks Jr. committed over the years, and the cost both in actual dollars and hours spent he, the father, had incurred.

So, when Lenny called his father that day he was uncertain exactly how the call would go.

"Lenny Franks please."

"Who's calling?"

"Lenny Franks."

He always got a bang out of that one.

"One moment…"

"Lenny?"

His father's voice boomed through thousands of miles of satellites and optics and wires.

"Yep it's me."

"What's going on?"

Lenny decided he'd just dive right in.

"Well she broke up with me and you already know how I am with the regular stories in my head and all and Teddy and I watched Castaway and we just can't be here anymore right now and with the stuff in my brain from the war and everything so I think I'm going to California to try and figure things out and see what the tide could bring."

Lenny Franks Sr. didn't say anything for a minute. Lenny figured he was calculating how many more checks he was going to have to write and how soon.

"Dad?"

"What are you going to do?"

"Well I'm not sure."

"Jesus. Jesus."

Lenny Franks Sr. said that a lot when he was considering what something was about to cost him.

"It's gonna be ok Dad. I got a little money put away and I think I can find something else to do. Maybe if you can spare a few bucks that would be really helpful."

Lenny actually had almost no money put away and absolutely no idea what he was going to do. He sure as hell didn't know he was going to try and save the human race, but even if he had, he would be sure that Lenny, Sr. wouldn't approve. Lenny Franks, Sr. was not a dreamer. He couldn't afford to be. He had too many checks to write.

"Lenny – you're such a talented guy – but I worry about you."

Lenny could hear his Dad fumbling with a file folder…

"I mean you had your bike stolen when you were 11 and you broke the garage window with the basketball the next fall and…

Lenny listened to his father run down the list from the ledger again.

… and then there was the boat and the big cellphone bill and the $ 400 tab at the club bar in December of 1985 and not understanding mortgage interest… well… you know… I just worry."

"It's ok Dad really it is."

"Look Lenny I'll give you a few bucks and I'll write it down and try not to fuck it up."

"Ok. Thanks Dad."

What more could either of em do really.

"Well listen. Just get over the girl and move on."

"Sure thing."

And Lenny hung up the phone and thought about the call. Actually, it went better than he thought, but he still knew Lenny Franks, Sr. presumed he was going to screw it all up. Like he did during the war. And Lenny decided not to argue with him about the part about just getting over the girl. It wasn't gonna be as simple as that, but this would be another notion his father wouldn't care to entertain.

Lenny couldn't blame him for thinking all those things when it got right down to it. The war was brutal and Lenny Franks, Sr. bore much of the cost and in more than just dollars. Lenny's dad thought he would be going to a funeral back in those days and that's hard on anybody. It was murder on Lenny, Sr., and even though he didn't say it, he sure acted like he never forgot about what Lenny had put him through over all those years. As Lenny held the phone in his hand he too thought about the war. He didn't do that usually because it hurt him like hell too, and maybe his Dad didn't think about that so much.

During the war, he lost things. And it wasn't a war the way you think of a war, like the Korean war, but if you almost die in a battle doesn't that count? He lost money and his car and his job and a lot of his brain probably. But he also knew Los Angeles wasn't the reason. In fact, Los Angeles kept calling him back for visits to clear his head. He thought about how badly he screwed things up there and he wished he had a do-over but nobody ever gets a do-over. He remembered living in that tiny little garage and watching things disappear. The stereo and the TV and the furniture all went out the door, so did his dishes and clothes and even the sailboat he won in a contest.

Lenny Franks, Sr. had this switch he could throw in his own brain to just forget about something and keep going with his life. Lenny Franks, Jr. had a smaller version of the switch and it didn't work all that great anymore. It wouldn't be easy to just move on with his life or forget about his girlfriend. It wouldn't be easy to figure out what was going to be next. Lenny Jr. didn't believe most of the stories in his head that others put there and he wasn't in the same business as Lenny, Sr. and didn't have the same head either.

That frustrated both of them greatly and on those points, they most certainly were of the same mind.

CHAPTER 6

Lenny Franks would ultimately lose the battle on behalf of the human race to beings from the planet *Banglordia,* so it's a good time to tell you more about who was gonna be in charge of earth after humans.

Banglordians were tall and narrow creatures about eleven feet high and ten inches wide and purplish in color. The males and females were identical except that the females had a second nipple. Why the males had even one, nobody really understood. They possessed keen intellects and keener senses of humor. They found joy in all things, as they and all advanced races were aware, that laughter was itself the fundamental ingredient to happiness and an enlightened society.

Females were also born pregnant and the males had no sex organs. This was a tremendous advantage over most species in the universe. Male *Banglordians* used absolutely no brainpower on thinking about sex or *Banglordian* females.

Imagine what that meant.

Some had different striping or darker or lighter coloring, but they all saw themselves as members of the same large cluster. Smaller clusters were formed and then modified and it was all quite arbitrary. And without the sexual component, these clusters mostly stayed together for their natural lives. Sometimes females would cluster with other females, or males with other males, or there would be several clustering together with new offspring. And it went like that. Sometimes young *Banglordians* found fellow *Banglordians* to cluster off and laugh with – and another cluster was formed.

In the history of the universe, it was true that most wars were fought, and most power struggles ensued, and even petty jealousies and squabbles were pretty much found only among races and on planets where the males had fully functioning penises or other sex organs. It really always was about that when you got right down to it. Take earth for one example.

Shelter and accommodations were built from sticks as needed. *Banglordians* did not require much sheltering and space in general, and they slept standing up and huddled together. Think of a really tall matchbook with really tall matchsticks. Now take away the matchbox and pretend the sticks were standing up by themselves. That's what it looked like.

Banglordians slept for about 2 hours at a time 3 times a day. They breathed regular oxygen but could breathe pretty much anything and they drank salt water (*Banglordia's* rain was salt water rain from salt clouds) and they ate plastic and rubber. They had impeccable digestive systems, and shat perfect tiny little yellow cubes that smelled like gardenias.

The rest of the time was spent primarily trying to make each other laugh and not think too hard. If given the choice wouldn't you rather be laughing and not thinking too hard? So that's what they did. There was no religion and no god and no money and nothing to buy and so nothing to argue about really.

Imagine what all that meant.

Every *Banglordian* counted the same, and they each counted hardly at all.

This is not to say that the civilization was without means. Oh – they had means alright. They were extremely advanced technologically, philosophically and in every way that mattered. They were just very highly evolved, and the higher you evolve, the less frequently you wear good clothes, and the fewer meetings you schedule, and email calendar invites you send, and the less shit you got lying around.

Life was pretty simple and pretty great if you were a *Banglordian*.

Banglordia was dying however as its second moon *Banglordia Zubie* (there were two -the other was *Banglordia Lehts)* had been struck by an enormous meteor and was beginning to disintegrate. This created great earthquakes and storms on the mother planet. They needed a new home.

The Banglordia High Counsel (a loosely formed group of elders thrown together after the meteor strike) tasked *Steven 22761* (yes, his first name was *Steven* - in a very odd coincidence *Banglordians* had many of the same first names as the people of earth, but their last names were numbers) to handle the assignment.

Steven 22761, and his cluster partner *Michael 51586,* attacked the issue with their usual diligence and fastidiousness and fashion sense. When the *Banglordians* had to get shit done for survival they were more than capable of getting shit done.

So, *22761* and *51586* got moving. First, they created a timeline calculating when their home world would be uninhabitable. Then working backwards from that deadline, they devised the plan and supervised the design and production of the great ships. The first was *BL-001* and would be ready for long range scouting missions very quickly. It was sleek and fast and modular, and it needed to be able to accommodate about half of the population in case their timeline was off and their world was destroyed before everyone was safely away.

BL-001 launched on *Z199001* by the earth calendar it was December 19, 1940. Some 500,000 ecstatic and giggling *Banglordian* souls took to the skies in their sleek new purple ship, that was equipped with the latest technology and plenty of foodstuffs and supplies and a digital log of their world. The ship was bedecked with bright colors all around the inside decks. That touch was provided by *Michael51586*.

The commander of *BL-001* was one *Rufus622* and he conducted a series of grid searches for possible alternative home worlds. This he did with mathematic precision. *622's* orders were to find a long-term home compatible with respect to atmospheric conditions, weather patterns and sources of food, and so on. By utilizing the considerable means at his disposal, he was to survey the universe and scout for a planet and secure it for colonization.

It should be mentioned here that the *Banglordians* had no military and hadn't needed one for millennia. They never had prior cause to leave their planet and there were no foreign invaders. *Banglordians* were a clever bunch though, and in the large conference room before the launch it was suggested to *622* that should he find the perfect place, but that the current inhabitants may be hostile, that he should assess their technological capabilities, and if necessary, nudge them toward their own demise. It was commonly known around the universe that young races getting cellphone technology too quickly was a surefire way to swift self-implosion.

The humans on Earth hadn't heard that one before.

After a couple of false starts *BL-001* stumbled through the Milky Way and happened upon Earth and all the preliminary observations were very promising. In his communiqué to his superiors after his second field recon mission, *622* laid it out quite accurately.

His plan was green-lighted immediately, and the wheels began to turn. *622* supervised casually dropping primitive *SNS1022* chips in Earth's most prominent and scientific cities. His crew set up monitoring devices all around the planet and the first test signal was beamed back to their home world almost right away. *The Banglordian High Counsel,* all assembled in the conference room, watched bombs exploding and humans jumping out of airplanes and humans slamming into each other in automobiles and later humans placing their hands under electronic restroom hand dryers. That one had them all laughing hysterically every time.

When the cellphone technology got into the mainstream and into almost every Earth's citizens' hands, *Banglordians* laughed so hard so regularly that they routinely shat themselves and this produced even more laughter. They all had quite the time - watching humans walking into

43

each other because they were staring at tiny screens in their hands –
watching humans dropping the tiny screens into toilets – watching
humans ignore each other completely more and more. They watched
humans tear up their own home and eat shit and drink shit. They watched
humans shoot each other and blow each other up some more and they
marveled at that because that's what humans were actually really good at.

Banglordians watched the people of Earth on big screens like
the people of Earth watched each other on their reality TV shows. Except
unlike the people of earth, *Banglordians* could watch for a few seconds
and then go on with their lives. And tracking humans, planting
suggestive messages in the technology, and messing with things like
voting and their money and credit and maps to go places (Phase II) was
made so much easier by the unexpected development of a network of
drink shops. These were among the first public places to proliferate
technology that enabled humans to sit on their asses in the same places,
and waste incalculable amounts of time while pumping more shit into
their bodies and looking at ridiculous images and then sending them
through the technology to each other. Humans were so easily distracted.
They hated real life. They craved distraction. Humans never paid
attention to the things humans really should be paying attention to. They
worried about all the wrong things. When humans started distracting
themselves while driving their automobiles and riding their bicycles the
fatalities skyrocketed.

44

The *Banglordians* also caught a break in regards to the gathering of

what would be the few remaining humans into collecting and shipping

stations, (Phase III) when they saw a vast string of large technology

stores with no pillars inside for easy stacking of humans. Incredibly,

humans would willingly line up and wait for days, and walk in with their

heads down for the next more expensive version of what they already had

in their hands.

And with the new idiot in charge of the most powerful human

cluster, more enormous bombs would be dropping soon.

The whole thing was a turkey shoot.

There was however an unforeseen problem with the *Banglordian*

SNS1022 chip technology that was eventually corrected. For a period of

about four months in early 1984, humans who lived in the western

hemisphere of the United States, and who ingested the right combination

of illicit chemicals could actually – if the angle and light and time of day

was just right – look into a mirror and see the *Banglordians* on their home

world observing the people of Earth and at various times both past and

future. It was, in laymen's terms, a quantum physics glitch in the

subprogram software.

It was what Lenny Franks thought was a series of drug induced

hallucinations but always thought maybe there was more to it than that.

Turns out there was.

Sal1111, the brightest *Banglordian* programmer and inventor of the *SNS1022* chip caught it and fixed the problem quickly. It was a very small number of humans however that had this experience and almost all of them wrote it off as part of their drug induced hallucinations.

When Lenny was in the hospital after the war and his time in LA in the early 1980's, he shared some very strange stories with some of the other humans there with him. His primary counselor had heard the rumblings and in a private session asked Lenny to lay it out for him.

The Counselor was a man named *Judge* who nodded politely and asked several follow up questions.

"Who's Ridgmont?"

"Oh, he's a guy I used to work for and snort cocaine with."

"How long do you suppose we have Lenny?"

"Now probably 50 years. Maybe less."

Lenny replied.

"Are you in communication with any of them?"

"Directly no. But wouldn't that be something?"

CHAPTER 7

The route Lenny Franks and Teddy planned to take, after watching Castaway, would take them out of Texas and across New Mexico, and then through Arizona and then Nevada, and then into California past the windmills to Los Angeles. He didn't want to think about the windmills part because windmills scared the shit out of him.

His Aunt Rita always told him he had two brains and that made as much sense to him as anything anybody else ever said as to why he was the way he was. He thought and thought and thought, and even ran the stories other people had told him over and over. He didn't believe em all but that's what was in there and it happened automatically. He wished he could stop all the stories sometimes and just have a break. Lenny could really chew on something until it was all chewed up, and then he'd start chewing on it some more.

After lunchtime on the new first official day of his new life Lenny was still sad. He had done so much with his life, he thought, but he told himself he had accomplished so little. Now he didn't know what he would do. Now he thought about her. He started chewing on her.

He didn't think he'd ever get married again and then he met her. It was the safest girl ever he decided because she was so much younger than he was. He sat behind her in a meeting room every day for three months and just got lost staring at the back of her neck. It was so beautiful. Long and slender and strong. He memorized her neck. He could see it in his mind whenever he wanted and he saw it again now. the first time he ever spoke to her he said

"You have a very beautiful neck."

She smiled at him and in that instant, he knew she was special and she was. The whole thing started off as fun. Then he fell in love with her. Then he thought she needed him to save her. She didn't really ask but that never mattered to Lenny. It's what he knew how to do. That's what he was good at. And he loved her so that's what he did. And she loved him too. She loved him all along and he knew it. She still did and he knew that too. But some things are too hard and maybe this was one of them. He hoped not. And Lenny had to get his brain around it. He was old and had been kicked in the balls a bunch. She was so young and hadn't been. He knew that no relationship was ever smooth and nothing was perfect, but you're with somebody because you don't wanna do life without em. She didn't know about that yet. Sometimes it's as simple and as hard as that.

The Ciera was running just fine, and even the air conditioner felt like it was working ok, which it did the faster the car went. He had his collection of audio cassettes, and *The Cure* tape was playing *Love Song*, which was one of his favorites, even though he always had a problem picturing the girl Robert Smith was probably singing about. Right now, it was Lenny singing with Robert Smith for his girl who was no longer his girl. Lenny cried some more. He'd be happy when the crying stopped that was for sure.

Lenny had a few maps and some scant lists because that's how Lenny used to be, but he decided that this time he wouldn't plan everything so hard. He always needed to know what would happen next. He was used to knowing what would happen next. He thought maybe he had to be ok not knowing what would happen next. Maybe he couldn't make everything happen the way he wanted. He told himself that every few minutes just to see if that helped stopped the crying.

"It's good to not know what's going to happen next."

He didn't believe it all at first, and he kept crying, but he kept saying it anyway.

He was no stranger to sleeping in his car and so he planned that when he got tired he'd sleep.

It wasn't his goal to be young again, but surprisingly, he felt young as he listened to his music and looked out the window at all the things there were to see.

The afternoons were the toughest part though because he had to pee all the time. He had gone to the Mayo clinic to check all that out one time and it turned out there wasn't much anybody could do. Of course, they could only tell him this after they put tubes up his pecker and his asshole and shot water up both holes. The nurses put electrodes all over his body, and everybody was looking at TV sets showing squiggly lines and bright yellow numbers.

The Doctor kept saying

"Do you follow me?"

when he was explaining it all. Here's what it was like:

"Your bladder is connected to your brain do you follow me?"

"And your brain signals your body to urinate do you follow me?"

"And in your case your brain and your bladder do you follow me? "

"Aren't talking to each other very well do you follow me?"

"And so, you're gonna pee all the time do you follow me?"

The doctor said.

Lenny followed him because he already knew all that stuff. When a guy pees thirty times a day, he figures his brain and his bladder might not be talking to each other so good. They gave him pills and asked him to fly to Rochester once a year to pee in a cup. He did that once and then called and asked them if maybe there was a cup in his home state he could pee into. So, he stopped going to Rochester and eventually stopped taking the pills too. And he even quit peeing into a cup once a year.

The best way to handle the whole thing was to not drink too much water and always keep an empty plastic Gatorade bottle in the car in case he had to pee. He got pretty good at driving and peeing into the plastic bottle. When he'd stop for gas Lenny would empty the bottle. It was a fine system.

Near the end of that first day it was getting dark and Lenny was tired. He saw a rest stop up ahead and pulled in and emptied the plastic bottle and went pee. He fetched the blanket from the trunk and pulled Teddy out of the backpack and lay down in the back seat. He closed his eyes and thought about his girl again and saw her neck as if she was sitting right in front of him in that meeting room. He closed his eyes and told himself it was really great not to know what was going to happen next even though he didn't believe it. And then he realized he had to go pee again.

CHAPTER 8

New Mexico was actually ok Lenny thought, even though there were supposed to be meth labs all over the place. He wanted to see em if one of his stories was right about it. His grandma used to call TV shows stories and he always liked that so he called TV shows stories. But Lenny didn't see any meth labs. He did see lots of painted rocks and different colored license plates and red dirt all over the place. They also had *IN-N-OUT BURGER,* which is where he had lunch that day, and boy was it ever good. Except his hands smelled after. He forgot to bring the lotion he used after he had hamburgers. Every few minutes he smelled his hands and shook his head.

And he had a better system for Teddy. At first, he had him in the backpack for safe keeping but he wanted him to enjoy the trip too. He sat Teddy up on top of the backpack on the passenger seat so he would be higher and could see stuff out the window. And when he would leave the Ciera to get gas or go Pee or empty the pee bottle or eat, he'd put Teddy back in the backpack for safe keeping.

At the *IN-N-OUT BURGER* he also saw more than one human with a tattoo and that got him thinking maybe he should think about getting one.

What kind of tattoo should he get is what Lenny thought about all the rest of that day, and it kept his brain from chewing on her while he and Teddy were driving through New Mexico.

If there was one thing Lenny Franks always liked it was words, and so he decided the tattoo should have words in it, like from a song or a book or a movie or something. He knew lots of poems and jokes and he even memorized directions for things like putting shelves together. He figured that the tattoo couldn't be too long though, and that it probably shouldn't be directions for putting things like shelves together.

Then he thought about where he might put the words. This was tricky business. He wanted to put the words someplace he could see em all the time, but not some place he couldn't keep the words private if he wanted to. *Where* he put em – would have to come after *What the words would be* he concluded.

He thought about books he read, and stories and movies he watched, and songs he listened to, and tried to find the exact right thing to tattoo. His mind drifted to thinking about her and it struck him how he was always thinking about her. He thought about this business of worrying about what everyone was thinking about. He scanned his memory and relived some of the times he became frustrated by just how dumb, incompetent, or infuriating humans could be. He considered why he always felt like nobody appreciated when he saved them. He thought about how important it was to try to forget about the stories and the past, and to not worry about what was gonna happen next. But everything kept getting scrambled up in his brain. So, he kept driving and listening to The Cure and the thought maybe he would use something from one of their songs. Except all their songs were so damned depressing and his new life shouldn't be so depressing.

He stopped at a gas station later in the day and filled up the Ciera and went to a regular bathroom to go pee and dump out his Gatorade bottle. He bought nuts and bottled water for dinner and then got back in the car. He wasn't too hungry because of everything that was happening and nuts made a fine meal anyway he thought.

He drove a considerable distance until oncoming lights and construction barrels finally did him in. He pulled into a rest stop and went straight to the business of washing up and emptying the pee bottle and peeing. It was while he was peeing that it hit him right in the face.

At eye level, right where he was standing and grunting to pee, (which he did pretty much every time he peed) was a graffiti line written in sharpie, and he knew he had his tattoo. He went back to the car and took Teddy out of the backpack and lay down in the backseat with him and started to close his eyes. He was content for the moment. For a millisecond, he was ok not knowing what would happen next. he smiled.

And then he heard the sound he hadn't heard in a long time. It was familiar and it was coming from deep inside the backpack in the front seat

It was his cellphone ringing. It was her.

Chapter 9

In the large conference room at the command center on *Banglordia,* and at the same time Lenny's cellphone started ringing, there was a gathering of the *Banglordian High Counsel.* Today's agenda items: the building of the second ship *BL-002* to evacuate the rest of the *Banglordians,* and potentially adjusting the timeline of the operation. Monitoring of the humans revealed they were far ahead of schedule with respect to their own demise.

622 had checked in with his latest report and it had been received with good humor. here is the translation:

"Ship smooth and undetected STOP cube disposal facilitator repaired and decks cleaned STOP So many cubes after mass laughing hysteria following viewing screen transmissions from and activity following largest human cluster leader's incoherent wild ramblings and human responses over last few microfledgers STOP Humans more mad at each other than ever STOP Every human spending more and more time isolated with tiny screens STOP Floods and Fires and Hurricanes and Earthquakes and shootings and bombings all over the place STOP.

Assume your monitoring and estimations in line with ours that schedule can be accelerated due to humans moving faster than anticipated toward compliance and conclusion STOP."

The room was lively as the chatter focused on the good news from *622* and the fun they were having watching the humans on earth stumblefuck their way to oblivion. They were happy of course but nobody was taking or giving credit or patting themselves or anyone else on the back. That wasn't how it was with *Banglordians*. They weren't accustomed to any displays of ego. In fact, only one asshole *Banglordian* was born in every 1.8 million births, and when it happened they just put him with the 3 other assholes on a huge island that had lots of plastic and saltwater rain.

Now they just laughed and laughed and shat more tiny cubes all over the conference room. And although they were pleased for what was happening now, they weren't thinking too hard, and no *Banglordian* was worried about what was going to happen next.

CHAPTER 10

It rained almost the whole next day and that always made Lenny feel a little sad and his armpits would hurt. As he continued along the highway, he turned over, inside out, upside down, and back again the conversation on the phone with her the night before.

When the phone rang last night, he got up from the backseat and jumped over the front seat and hit his nuts on the center console. Life was always kicking you in the nuts. He dug the phone out of the backpack and held it in his hand and saw her name flashing. For a moment considered not picking it up. He'd gotten away and hadn't spoken to anyone. He thought he had turned his phone off. He was done with the damned thing more and more, and felt more strongly than ever that these things would be the end of us all but he kept it anyway.

I probably kept it and left it on because it meant the connection with her was still possible

is what he thought.

Although he missed her terribly and loved her still, he didn't know if talking to her right now was such a good idea. He was fragile, and he knew enough to know that when you're fragile you do things you might not normally do. You say things you might not normally say. But life is fucking hard and terrifying. There aren't so many hard and fast rules for this kind of thing and in his heart, he knew he wanted to hear her voice.

"Don't think too much and don't worry about what's gonna happen next" he said aloud as he pushed the button.

"Hello"

"Hi Lenny…"

"Hi…"

"How ya doin?"

"I'm good I'm Good…"

Lenny always repeated himself when he was nervous.

"I'm good too…"

It was strange to hear her voice because the last time he heard it his world exploded. The things that come out of a call like that last one hit you like a shovel to the face. One of the very hardest thwacks came in that painful instant when she said goodbye and she intended it to finally be goodbye. He thought

– here's my girl – MY girl – who a moment ago - just a few seconds ago really - would give herself to me and me alone ... and right now in this terrible moment she's telling me she would give herself to anyone else in this world or any other except me.

That she opened his brain up to think about it like that, and that his brain did think about it like that was almost too much to bear. He thought she couldn't have meant it like that, could she? He reasoned with himself that she was just young and scared and had too many things going on in her own life. He didn't really start thinking yet about what a pain in the ass he could be to be around but that would come. It's hard to know exactly how to behave as a boyfriend or husband. All you had on the subject were the stories you heard from other people and what you saw in person or on TV. His brain was chewing and chewing and chewing on the last call as they spoke.

The awkward small talk continued. At one point Lenny didn't know if he was even there or if he was just observing this other person speaking back to her. He was nervous. His palms were sweating. He knew hers were too because she had this thing where your palms sweat a lot. He liked that about her. It made her even more special he always thought. He loved her hands too even though she wasn't particularly fond of them. He thought about her hands now. He didn't want to say the wrong thing. It was like trying to navigate a minefield in heavy steel boots. They talked about this and about that and finally they got around to the fact that he wasn't in her same city anymore.

"Oh goodness Me…"

She said.

She was very young but she talked like a seventy-year-old woman. Lenny always smiled when she said things like that and he smiled now.

"I just had to get out of there. To be honest there's a lot of reason's but I couldn't be in that apartment anymore because I kept running into you every place."

It's true and it was pretty common for people when things like this happened.

She spent considerable time there for about a year and so he kept finding Easter Eggs like clothes, shampoo, a toothbrush, or a jacket that she left or mislaid or forgot in every corner and cabinet and drawer and closet. There was even the sticker on the ceiling and what that's about is gonna stay between them.

The hardest part of breaking up, Lenny thought, was how to handle all the memories and reminders, and that little apartment was busting with em and it was driving him crazy. And in the new age you couldn't just tear the photos up and throw them in the trash. They were on your phone and computer forever. The thought of going in there to try to get rid of them was too much to consider. Of course, there was the exercise itself of having to look through all the smiles and the handholding and all that all over again, which was for sure painful, but then there was the technological challenge of getting rid of them forever. The guy at the store or on the phone or the robot on the chat thing would always tell you how easy it is and it never ever was that easy. Not ever. Not even once.

"Oh Lenny... I miss you..."

And there it was.

HOPE.

That most dangerous and wonderful and lovely and potentially destructive and fatal feeling of them all. That last thing that lingered inside Pandora's box after the fucking lid slammed shut. That most comforting friend and cruelest foe. **HOPE** always starts with an imaginary flicker. A phantom wisp. A single slight caught breath. Then it gets stronger because you feed it and make it stronger. But as strong as it gets it can be snuffed out so very quickly at any time, for **HOPE** does not really exist in the physical world. It's a construct. A ghost. An illusion. **HOPE** isn't real but in that moment, it's all you have and so you make it so real. You hang on to it like you're going under and it's the last log in the river. And In that moment Lenny strapped himself to **HOPE** thinking it could put it all back the way it used to be. He sensed she wanted it too. Or was that just what **HOPE** did to a guy. or a girl.

"I miss you too… and I LOVE you."

That was the biggest risk of all and he held his breath for what seemed like a million years and waited for her response.

"I Love You Too Lenny."

She said it quietly but with what Lenny felt was complete sincerity. In his gut, he had known she felt that way and never stopped feeling that way. He knew it! He knew it! He knew it!

And that swelled his **HOPE**. And Hers. Just a flicker, maybe a little more. But Fragile. Tenuous. Strong like titanium you thought, but brittle like a robin's eggshell you knew, at the same time. They were careful with each other that night. Neither one of them offering too much or getting too close for fear of smothering **HOPE** and putting it out for once and all. Neither of them wanted that right then. The truth is that they both were deeply in love still. They both missed each other. They both needed each other. It ended because she didn't know where she was going and he was already there. It ended because he was impatient and a pain in the ass and she was trying to find her way. Love survives that of course, but could they? It might end, but it's not supposed to end now, Lenny believed.

They laughed and talked and settled in a bit and then said their goodbyes and Lenny pressed the button to hang up. How he felt was hard to describe. But this was clear in his head –

he was really, really thinking too hard and wondering what the hell was going to happen next.

CHAPTER 11

Sometimes in books you'll get introduced to a new character kinda right out of the blue and this is one of those times. Anyway, you can probably use a break after the heavy stuff in the last chapter.

Actually, you heard about Patch – or at least it was mentioned that Patch who would become Lenny Frank's best friend in the world. So, while Lenny rumbles down the highway trying not to think about what's going to happen next, here's the guy he has absolutely no idea he's about to run into.

It's funny if you think about it.

If Lenny looked back on it he never ever knew what was about to happen next and what wonderful moment was about to occur. Who was gonna walk through that door? Who was gonna be on the other end of the phone? A guy gets so caught up in thinking about what *has* happened or worrying about what *will* happen, and then life just kinda puts something right in his lap. And wouldn't you know it, but did Lenny ever have a lot of extraordinary things just pop up around him. If he had taken five minutes to think about this concept, it might have struck him that even on those days and at those crucible times, he never had any feeling in advance that that was in fact the day. That that was going to be the moment. That that was going to be the person who changed his life extraordinarily. So, if he had thought about it for five minutes maybe he wouldn't have worried at all. Why should he think so hard about everything or worry at all? In fact, why shouldn't Lenny Franks be jumping up and down about every second, happy about what the next one could bring? All the evidence pointed to him having extraordinary moments happening again and again and again. If he just wasn't so fucking worried about what the hell was gonna happen next. And he was about to meet who would become next to Teddy about the best friend a guy could ever have.

Turns out it was a hell of a story and a hell of life Patch had, which probably doesn't surprise you at all. If you've been around, you know that people with crazy, extraordinary lives seem to bump into each other all the time. You don't have to read this particular story if you don't want to but it's good background on Patch, and Lenny is gonna meet Patch in a few chapters so this will give you a head start.

Patch and Lenny Franks were about the same age but after that is pretty much where the story stops matching up.

Patch is a black man and was born in New Orleans. He had an older sister who still lived there but he hadn't seen her in years. She was still there working on designing bicycles.

His Mom died when he was young and his Dad did about the best he could, including dressing up like a woman for extra money, but Patch didn't like to talk about that part and who can blame him really. His Dad mostly worked where they put hard plastic cases on things like scissors and knives.

When Patch was really little, he got a piece of a pencil from a lawnmower shot in his eye so he had to wear an eye patch for the whole summer. That's how he got the name Patch and it stuck. His real name was Eugene which never seemed to fit too good anyway.

Patch left home when he was 15, not because he was mad or anything, but because he didn't want his Dad to worry about spending money he didn't have on him. Patch's older sister was smart in school, and Patch figured that his Dad should concentrate on the horse with the best chance of winning. That's how Patch always said it on the few times he told the story.

Patch went from job to job and kept heading west until he wound up in Chicago, where he worked as a bouncer at a bar where the girls took their tops off and danced. All he said about that was he never got to see many titties because he mostly had his back to them to keep an eye on the riff raff.

But it paid ok and Patch could make more money by taking some of the girls home or to their boyfriend's' house or to other guys houses in his car. If you've been around at all you know what that means.

There was one dancer Patch really liked and she liked him and it just killed him to give her rides to guys houses. But that was how it was until one night, there was trouble, and all Patch would say about that was the guy probably didn't eat solid food for a couple of months. He and the gal split that night.

The girl's name was Jenny and she was white and had short hair most of the time and titties that god himself must have personally inspected before sending them out is how he would put it. And Patch would laugh when he'd tell the story. He and Jenny had quite a time, and drove all the way to Denver in a piece of shit old Bronco that he had and they got married and had a baby boy.

But Patch knew he could never keep a girl like that around for too long, and sure enough he couldn't. Patch and Jenny got divorced, but he hung around Denver so he could visit Joshua who was his son.

The guy Jenny married was named Pete, and he was actually ok for a white guy is how Patch would say it. Pete even offered Patch a job at his car battery store, but Patch was too proud to do that. He worked here and there and started sleeping outside when he didn't have money to pay the rent. He hung around Denver and kept a set of good clothes in a bag so that when he went to see Joshua he would look like a real Dad.

Patch was on welfare and food stamps for a while, but when that was over and he couldn't find a job because he wasn't that good at anything, he almost gave up. But he kept Putting on the good clothes once a week to visit Joshua and that kept him going.

One day when he was wandering around Denver when it was really cold, he came to a church where some guys were building a garage in the back. He was sort of hanging around when one of the guys who turned out to be the Priest, and his name was Father Mark, said do you know anything about building a garage? Patch said no, and Father Mark said well maybe it's time you learned. That started Patch's short career in the construction business. Patch worked for Father Mark and the church that was called Our Holy Lady. Our Holy Lady was unaffiliated with any real religion, and there were always big guys showing up and giving Father Mark envelopes with lots of money in them. Patch minded his own business, but thought it was weird. He also wondered what the deal was with all the girls with big titties dropping by, but he figured that maybe they were trying to find God.

Father Mark was really good to Patch. He taught him how to close his eyes to talk to GOD, or clear his head. He let him sleep in the garage when it was done, and paid him more than Patch thought he should. Father Mark brought him food, and Patch would even bring Joshua with him on Sundays. Every now and then Father Mark would ask Patch to go on an errand with him, and that meant standing next to Father Mark when he went to pick up more donation envelopes. Everything was really good for a long time for Patch. He was fixing this and fixing that and helping people who went to the church when they needed something built. Father Mark was paying him and being nice to him and taught him about God and how everything happens for a reason.

Patch liked that and used it all the time after that.

He'd say things like

"Ain't this the best world we got?"

and

"Ain't this proof that everything happens for a reason?"

One night though there was all this noise and when Patch came out of the garage in his underwear, the police were there and they were arresting Father Mark for loansharking and prostitution and selling drugs.

All Patch ever said about that was everything happens for a reason.

Chapter 12

Lenny drove on through New Mexico trying not to worry about what would happen next with his girl. His brain was fairly occupied anyway because he now knew what the tattoo would say. He saw on the big green road signs with the miles on them that the town called Tucumcari was coming up. He wondered if maybe they had a store where he could buy his tattoo.

The last few miles before Tucumcari, he was excited, but nervous.

"Teddy it's a good idea, isn't it?"

"Teddy maybe I should get you one too?"

"Teddy where should we put it?"

"Damn my armpits hurt Teddy."

Lenny took the off ramp and pulled into Tucumcari. He worked the Ciera into the first gas station and pumped the gas and went inside. He felt good. He even got out of his comfort zone and asked the guy behind the counter if there were any stores in Tucumcari that sold tattoos. He was as helpful as the guys at the hardware store back home. Some day he thought, maybe, just maybe, somebody would actually be able to answer a simple question with a simple and correct answer.

Lenny got back in the car and drove around town looking for a store that sold tattoos. After driving around for a bit, he found a parking place and decided to do the rest of the search on foot. It was a clearing up and he liked to walk.

Lenny decided he liked Tucumcari. There weren't a lot of cars and there seemed to be fewer humans per capita with their faces screwed into their cellphones. Nobody seemed to be in too big a hurry.

He turned the corner and walked down a street with little stores where they sold things like jewelry with rocks instead of diamonds, Indian dolls but not from India, and lots of things with beads and feathers. Finally, he saw a store that was called *Pigs Tattoos* and he figured he could maybe get his tattoo there but you never really know until you go inside a place.

The door was held open with a big rock and as soon as Lenny went inside and looked around he figured that this was the place. There were pictures of tattoos everywhere and there were stations with tools that looked like drills to Lenny. The only soul in the place was a pretty woman with a tight-fitting T-shirt with some kind of an oriental design on it. But all he looked at was her huge breasts that were stretching the T-shirt till he thought it would pop.

"What can I do you for?"

The woman with the huge breasts said to Lenny. He figured that's what she said to every new human who walked in.

"Hi. I used to be Lenny Franks. My girlfriend broke up with me and I'm trying not to think about what happens next and I thought I might get a tattoo."

"Well Hi Lenny Franks you poor thing. I'm still Eva and I think a tattoo is a marvelous idea."

"Is *Pig* here?"

Eva laughed.

"Sweetie, if you wanna see *Pig* you're gonna have to go to the cemetery."

"Oh, I'm sorry about that."

Lenny said.

"Don't be sorry. *Pig* was a fucking asshole. And he was a shitty businessman. And Lenny – pardon my French – he was lousy in the sack."

Lenny thought about the phrasing on that one.

"But the name had some value so I kept it."

Eva said.

"Oh. So, you're *Pig* now?"

Lenny asked.

Lenny was closer than he knew.

In truth, she *was Pig* now.

This is another part of the book where you don't have to read this part if you don't want to, but this is a funny story, so maybe give it a go.

The real *Pig,* aka William Brigham, aka Billy Briggs, aka Bill Braggs, was a small-time dumbfuck who rode with a biker gang from Northern California called *The Sand Knights* in the early 2000's. His moniker *Pig* came not from his own physical appearance, he was tall and slight, but from the type of women he seemed to favor.

Most of *Pig's* public transgressions, and the gangs for that matter were smalltime – assaults, public intoxication, public urinating, and the odd burglary or petty theft. *Pig* did a little time which were mostly 30 and 60 day hitches in county jails across the Southwest before he pulled what was at the time the biggest robbery in Albuquerque, New Mexico's history.

The Sand Knights took down two armored trucks on a cross-state transport route in broad daylight on May 15, 2001. The plan was ill conceived from the get go with the only issue in question was whether *Pig* and *The Sand Knights* would be captured or shot dead.

Carl *Cockbite* Cocharan shared his plan with his fellow *Knighters* after a long night of drinking beer and smoking marijuana. *Pig,* who had heard about it earlier from *Cockbite,* enthusiastically supported the idea in front of the group as they had agreed in advance.

"It's perfect."

Cockbite said to his compatriots.

"*Philly* Philson went straight and now is a guard for the transport company. He's gonna fake car trouble for us – and when he gets out to check we're going to ambush him and force his buddies to get out and open the trucks."

After what *Pig* would later admit to being extremely cursory vetting of the details of *Cockbite's* plan, and even less discussion about how to physically transport palates of cash on the backs of motorcycles, the group organized and setup for the robbery.

The Sand Knights hid their choppers behind desert boulders at the specified highway mile marker and waited for *Philly* Philson and his small armored motorcade. They got the day wrong however, and wound up spending the night drinking what little booze they had and almost freezing to death in the New Mexico desert.

The next day *Philly* Philson, driving the first of the two armored trucks did his bit and stopped the first armored truck at the agreed upon spot. When *Philly* Philson got out of the truck and went to the hood, *Cockbite* led the charge grabbed *Philly* Philson around the neck and put his 38 up to *Philly* Philson's temple. The others, including *Pig,* trained their weapons on the other armored truck guards who were locked in their respective trucks.

"OK – open the back of the truck!"

Cockbite barked.

Philly Philson said

"I don't have the keys - they're inside with Douglas."

"Well tell that cocksucker Douglas to get out here and open the back of the truck"

After a very long standoff that was settled only when *Cockbite*, in an unexpected display of the seriousness of his request, shot his good friend *Philly* Philson dead in the temple the guards started moving.

Douglas and Edwards and Gorsievski, the three remaining guards, slowly worked their ways out of their vehicles, in large part to knowing that their radio calls for police and federal backup had been answered and that help would be there in only a few moments.

Cockbite and *Pig* and the rest of *The Sand Knights* got as far as getting most of the palates out of the two trucks and to the highway. They had managed (by the final total that would not be made public) to be in possession of a little over $ 3,700,000 in cash for approximately twenty-five seconds before the police and feds got there and arrested the perpetrators without firing a single shot.

Cockbite got 20 years for second-degree murder and another 20 for his role in the robbery. The rest, including *Pig,* were quick to roll over on *Cockbite* and received average sentences of 10-15 years. Douglas and

Edwards and Gorsievski each got $ 500.00 bonuses from their employers and certificates of heroism from the industries' top trade magazine *Hard Armor Monthly*.

The contents of *Philly* Philson's work locker were inspected and then incinerated. Having no family or friends other than *Cockbite*, *Philly* Philson was also incinerated and his ashes were shoveled into a drain in the back of the funeral home.

Pig actually had a fine career in prison, and it was helped by his befriending a man named John Gordon Levine, who was doing 5 years for tax fraud. Levine had real estate holdings all over the Southwest including a tattoo shop in Tucumcari, New Mexico. Levine needed protection and cigarettes and *Pig* was found to be quite useful in both regards. He was slight but scrappy, and knew a lot of guys on the inside. And he had a reputation for not taking any shit.

They negotiated that as long as nothing happened to Levine while he was there, and as long as he was released without incident, he would transfer ownership of *Tucumcari Tattoo* to *Pig* when he was released. Levine made it through his sentence almost completely unscathed. His anus was not penetrated, and he was forced to perform oral sex on another inmate only twice while in the joint, both times when

Pig had been in the infirmary. *Pig* successfully argued on each occasion that he could not be held responsible since he was not on the cellblock.

And so, on July 12, 2005, John Gordon Levine kept his end of the bargain and transferred title of *Tucumcari Tattoo* to one William Brigham who was still incarcerated. On September 18, 2009 *Pig* was released for good behavior suffering only from chronic bladder infections as a result of trying to hold his urine too long out of boredom.

When *Pig* got out he showed up at *Tucumcari Tattoo* and, waiving the title to the store, informed the woman behind the counter that the place was his, and that it was to be called *Pig's Tattoo,* and that he'd show up every week to collect the profits.

Eva put up the sign and gave *Pig* an envelope every week for two years. Just to keep the peace while she waited for her ship to come in, she occasionally had intercourse with him. It was hardly any trouble given both the size of *Pig's* genitalia and the time it required for him to finish the task.

Then in December of 2011 Eva's ship did come in with the news that William *Pig* Brigham was accidentally run over by a vacationing armor truck driver named Marcus Douglas who just happened to be in the area. Nobody cared enough to make the connection.

Pig was dead and had the title and that was just fine with Eva. She had nothing to lose, no exposure, and no more envelopes to hand to anybody and no more tiny penises to entertain. She could run the place however she liked. Nobody followed up on the matters of *Pig's* estate. Eva correctly assumed that not a soul existed who gave a rats' ass.

So yes… Eva was *Pig*.

"Ha. That's a good one Lenny! Better than you even know!"

Lenny told her the story about trying to come with what the tattoo was gonna be. How he thought about pictures and shapes and numbers but that he settled on words. Except that he had trouble coming up with exactly what words.

"And then Eva when I was standing there going pee last night at the rest stop before the phone call and I saw it - I saw it on the wall – and – even though I don't believe in signs or anything – I really liked what it said."

Lenny said.

"What did it say Lenny?"

"It said - The lion does not concern himself with the opinions of sheep."

He finished with a flourish and extended his hands in the air and waited for the applause.

"It's Homeric you know. Achilles before his battle with Hector."

Eva said.

Lenny was really impressed with Eva and not just because of her large breasts that he could see most of, but he wished she had had a better reaction. He wished that a lot around humans. Especially women. They never quite reacted the way you wanted them to. He considered rolling that into all the things he had to work on.

Then Eva asked Lenny where he wanted the tattoo.

"Well – someplace where I can see it all the time if I want."

Eva stepped closer to Lenny and reached out and gently grabbed his right arm.

"Well Lenny…"

Eva said as she started turning his arm this way and that.

"How about on the inside of your forearm? That way you could always see it if you wanted and cover it with a shirt if you had to."

Next to his girl who maybe was still broken up with him, Eva was the smartest woman Lenny had met in a long time. And even though he liked the idea it was hard not to be distracted by her large breasts. He let her keep holding onto his arm and hoped it would last a long time. At the end of the day, *a man was only a guy*, Lenny thought.

"Lenny? What do you think? Lenny??"

Eva said.

It took him a minute and then he snapped out of it and said

"Sounds perfect. Except – maybe we could do it on the left arm?"

Lenny was a little afraid of an infection, and since he was right-handed he didn't want to chance it, in case they had to amputate.

"The left it is Lenny."

Eva said and then let go of Lenny's arm.

"C'mon Lenny – on the table you go."

Eva said.

Lenny took off his backpack and put it on the floor next to the table, fastening the strap around the table leg. He turned his head up toward Eva and said

"Will it hurt?"

Eva laughed.

"Oh Lenny – a big strong guy like you can handle it."

Lenny thought he might be getting a hard on and part of the problem over the years was he was really good at getting hard ons. Partially to distract himself and partially because he was nervous he asked Eva if Teddy could watch.

"Who's Teddy?"

Eva asked.

"Oh, he's my best friend in the world probably. I mean he's been there for all of it and he's never taken any pieces or anything. And he'd probably like to see it."

Lenny said.

"Why Lenny, I'd love that."

Lenny pulled Teddy out and showed him to Eva.

"Well hello Teddy I'm Eva."

"He can't talk or anything."

Lenny said.

"But I bet he's a great listener."

Eva said.

Lenny lay on the table and held Teddy in his right arm and Eva got to work soaping and cleaning his left. Lenny just smiled at Teddy. It was good to have a friend around for times like this.

Eva got the drill or whatever it was out, and went to work. As she etched the words on the inside of Lenny's arm, Lenny looked back and forth between Teddy and Eva's huge breasts which actually rubbed against him every now and then.

Lenny told Eva about his girl and she said to him that relationships can look any way two people want em to look. She also said that he was so sweet she couldn't imagine any girl not being in love with him, and he said oh you'd be surprised. But Lenny got a little excited because he realized that Eva was actually a nice woman to be around and she was talking to him. When you get broken up with, you wonder if there are ever gonna be any other nice women to be around who will talk to you. Eva helped him think that maybe there are other women out there if it actually came to that which he hoped it wouldn't.

If you asked Lenny about it later, he would say the tattooing didn't hurt too much and that it sort of tickled but not in the way that made you laugh.

Eva smiled and said it was time to talk about the damage, Lenny didn't know what she meant and actually got a little scared. She sensed this, so she said it was time for him to pay so they went to the counter together.

Eva wrote something down on this little pad.

"OK Lenny Franks, you also need this lotion to keep the tattoo nice and so it doesn't get infected."

"Does it work on your hands for after *IN-N-OUT Burgers*?"

Lenny said.

"You're welcome to try it." Eva said.

"Ok Lenny – that'll be two-forty."

"Two-forty what?"

"Two hundred and forty dollars. Without the tip, of course."

Lenny just about fainted. She was right when she said about the damage. But Lenny didn't want to look like one of those guys who was cheap, so he pulled out his wallet with the cash inside and gave her three one hundred dollar bills.

"Lenny – that's an awfully generous tip – 60 dollars! You didn't have to do that.

Eva said.

He hadn't but apparently, he did.

"You're welcome Eva."

Lenny said.

"And Teddy it was awfully nice to meet you too."

"He doesn't talk."

Eva put 100 dollars in the drawer and added 200 dollars to the growing pile in the safe in the back room. Four or five more years thought Eva and she could head to the Dominican Republic.

Lenny had his tattoo and was very excited that he was well on the way with his new life, whatever the hell it was gonna look like. He was smiling and happy and listening to The Cure and talking to Teddy and was feeling great about himself.

"I'm *THE LION* now Teddy. And here's the thing – even if they think I'm really good or really bad – *THE LION* doesn't have to listen to what *THE SHEEP* have to say about anything."

Lenny said.

Oh, Lenny was feeling pretty good about his new tattoo and his new outlook on life, and it took him to some important reflection going back to the war and then following through with what he had been through since and lately and everything else.

That's coming next but you might like to know because it's funny that It only took him about 100 times looking at the tattoo to realize she left the S off the word *opinions* on the tattoo.

Chapter 13

When Lenny was young he did drugs, and drank. A lot. He didn't care so much about himself and what he got into. And what he got into was like a trip to hell. That's what everybody figured he meant about the war and mostly that was right. They didn't know all about it for sure and he kept most of the craziest and saddest and shittiest details mostly to himself. Other than mentioning it the one time to his boss in those days, John Ridgmont, from whom he got a very tepid response, he never said much at all regarding the hallucinations with the tall skinny alien people who gave humans cellphones and were watching them fuck the whole thing up. Lenny assumed quite correctly that most humans would have absolutely no idea what to do with information like that.

The bulk of the war happened in Los Angeles and he was heading back that way.

Almost all humans would probably say

"Boy Lenny are you sure it's a good idea for you to go back there?"

Because that's how humans thought about things. They were always worried about what bad thing that would almost never happen might happen. He was very sure none of them would think stopping in Las Vegas would be a good idea.

He even used to make speeches about how bad the war was, and it was bad but now he wasn't so sure he knew what the hell he was even talking about. And humans would still always call him and ask him to give speeches about the war or talk to friends of theirs about the war. They didn't have much of an appreciation for what a pain in the ass it was for Lenny to talk about the war.

Lenny still didn't drink or use cocaine anymore but he drank caffeine and ate sugar and took pills the doctors said were ok. He had white pills and blue pills and yellow pills. He figured it was just a matter of time till they gave humans pills to stop drinking, and that they'd even make it available in a liquid form, and nobody would catch the irony. And Lenny even smoked pot every now and then. Every now and then means about 10 times or something over the past year before she broke up with him. They'd get stoned and eat ice cream and horse around like couples do and Lenny found it all quite wonderful.

He'd say he'd changed a lot since the war. But humans are funny and they see you how you show em to see you and how it works best for THEM to see you. It helped most humans to think that other humans had trouble with things they didn't think they had trouble with themselves. And most of the humans he knew usually asked him about the war when they were drinking wine so there was that.

Like his old human friends Vinnie and Babs would say things like

"Don't take even one drink or you know what will happen."

Lenny would nod and say thanks but think

Talk to me sometime about this stuff when you're not drinking wine which'll be hard because it's pretty much every time I see ya.

See Lenny was one of these all in or full stop guys his whole life. Black or White. People told him that's how he was and he thought that's how he was and he was but damn there's gotta be some grey doesn't there? People live in grey. And so, it was time for Lenny to start believing that he was actually living in the grey lots of times but that he hadn't noticed. And further, it would be more than possible going forward that he could live in more and more grey. It was time for him to remember that 26-year-old Lenny and 56-year-old Lenny really weren't the same guy. 56-year-old Lenny could do whatever the fuck he wanted to and look at the world anyway he chose.

Especially now with everybody on earth including Lenny running out of time and everything. Because the truth of the matter is that when what your boss, and the TV, and your Dad, and Vinnie and Babs, or anybody says doesn't matter to you so much, it's way easier. People worry about the craziest things after all. They're afraid of everything. EVERYTHNG. They get told every day what to be afraid of and how to be because they're going through this same business of listening to everybody else. Like when everybody ran out of gas when there was plenty of gas. They are, almost all of them, looking into their tiny screens all day long and lots of times they just care about videos of cats and sports and what they're told to be scared of, and not about their own health or their own existence or poor people. So, fuck em. Stop listening to em except on matters of cat videos or sports and even then, don't check your brain at the door.

And When you say fuck em and don't listen that anybody else thinks about YOU you're free to do life any way you want to, and then you're finally taking a lot of the trash out of your head. Because when it gets right down to it everybody – your boss and the TV and your Dad and Vinnie and Babs or even your girl sometimes or anybody else change their minds a lot because that's what humans do. What they think today isn't what they thought yesterday or will or might think tomorrow. And if you heard them in your head from yesterday or 10 or 50 years ago or today or tomorrow you live your life like that. So, what the fuck was the point of worrying about it? Why be like a stupid kite just getting blown all over the place by whichever way somebody else's wind is blowing? Fuck that Lenny thought and he got mad about it. Maybe today they think you're great and maybe tomorrow they're mad at you and what's the truth then? Maybe today they love you and maybe tomorrow they're scared. They told you and you believed them about what yesterday was and what tomorrow would be. You saw yourself through how they saw you and you got so used to it you wound up running your life and your world with those pictures and words in your head. You knew what would happen next because they and you told yourself what would happen next. You were trying to make something happen to fit the stories instead of just allowing it to happen and experiencing it for what it was. Worrying about what they thought, and what was gonna happen next, had actually played more of a role in Lenny's life than he had previously acknowledged or had ever thought about. He was sure he needed to forget about all that stuff and laugh a lot more.

The tattoo was right. And Lenny was gonna start living more like the tattoo said starting right fucking here and right fucking now.

Chapter 14

BL-002 was ready for deployment and the *Banglordian High Counsel* was tidying up the final business to evacuate the planet and load the remaining *Banglordians* and supplies aboard. You won't be surprised to learn that this process was unlike anything you might see on earth. Like for example anytime you were at the airport and watched humans get on an airplane maybe you thought to yourself, *dear god why is this the most disorganized clusterfuck of a thing when it really shouldn't be all that difficult.*

Well, the *Banglordians* just took their time and shuffled up toward the ship over a period of earth weeks. They laughed and shat yellow cubes. They sucked on rubber and ate plastic and drank seawater from large bins that were all over the place. They slept standing up and were absolutely unconcerned about their place in line, or when the ship would depart, or when they would get to their new planet. That sort of thing would have been pointless because time would keep moving all by itself and as it moved along they'd all find out what the deal was. All they had was the step they were taking and so they decided to laugh while taking each step. It was a simple choice really of what they wanted to do. Humans were more like stupid kites if you wanna know the truth about it.

The trip to their new home would take about 3 earth months give or take and that depended on whether or not they saw something interesting and wanted to stop and take a look. It would go like this:

They had these huge windows they could look out and if they wanted to laugh at something other than humans crashing into stuff they'd all make the same noise and it would sound like sheep bah-bah-bahing, and if it got loud enough, *BL-002* would automatically stop and circle. It was a fine system.

So, it happened then at about the same time that Lenny was nearing Las Vegas, Nevada, *BL-002* packed with the last *Banglordian* cleared its moorings and left its old home en route to rendezvous with *BL-002* and head together to their new home for colonization.

And just a few moments after leaving the bah-bah-bahing got very loud and the ship pivoted, and every *Banglordian* took a spot to look out one of the big windows and watch *Banglordia-Zubie* implode. The home planet of *Banglordia* would follow in just a few earth days, and every *Banglordian* laughed because they realized how fortunate they were to be all together and all able to laugh.

CHAPTER 15

On the way toward Las Vegas, Lenny chewed on the most recent

phone call with her. They were talking every couple of days now and he

was confused about that. He loved talking to her. He loved that they

were back talking with each other. But he kept wondering if she was

gonna get scared and run away again. If it was up to him they'd be

together now and see where they were at. But he knew it wasn't up to

him. Or was it? He wanted to see her but he had stuff to do, and she was

all the way back there with stuff to do. He tried to not worry about what

was gonna happen next. That by the way is way harder than it sounds.

She said to him on the last call

"How are you my love?"

And

"You're my guy."

And

"You know you're the sweetest kindest man I know and you're still

my very handsome man."

Those things made him feel better, hell, they'd make anybody feel better, and he thought he felt better because of the other reasons too. But did he feel better because he was actually better because he was thinking about himself and the world in new ways and not worrying about what would happen next? Or did he feel better because she was talking to him again? Lenny figured probably correctly that it was a little of both. The breakup was so dramatic and sudden and when it happened it was like his chest exploded into a million pieces. And it didn't feel at all like they were done yet. The pain of not being with each other was too great for them both. The thought of seeing each other again was wonderful. They held tightly onto those things. They held onto the good things and they worked harder at making each other feel OK. That was enough for now Lenny thought.

But what would happen if...

What would happen when...

Put that stuff away he told himself. Drive. Look out the windows. Ahead there would be a big distraction. Distractions help Guys Like Lenny Franks who have trouble trying not to worry about what was gonna happen next.

Just driving into Las Vegas and seeing all the lights on full blast distracted Lenny and made his heart excited, but at least one of his two brains was pretty nervous about the whole thing.

Las Vegas had changed a lot since the last time Lenny had been there. One of the ways it really changed was all the traffic, and the streets that you couldn't go on anymore. Not that he had ever driven there before, because when he went to Las Vegas he either walked or got in a taxicab. And now while driving on Las Vegas Boulevard, he realized he had to go pee pretty bad and the Gatorade jug was full. He found himself trapped in a long line of cars. He was about the twentieth car in line at a red light that looked like it let two cars through at a time.

He looked at Teddy and said

"I tell ya what Gif – this might be a problem."

Lenny loved Howard Cosell who used to start everything he said on Monday Night Football with I'll tell ya what Gif... So, Lenny would say it a lot and he thought Teddy liked hearing it.

He was on the right side of the street and there was a homeless guy leaning on a post. He was holding a piece of cardboard that said HOMELESS on it and it looked like it was written on there with color crayons.

Since the passenger doors were welded shut and their windows wouldn't roll up or down, Lenny couldn't figure out how to get a homeless dollar to the guy with the sign. Lenny always had homeless dollars in his car and he liked to give em to homeless humans. But Lenny kept looking at the homeless guy who kept looking at Lenny. Lenny smiled through the window and made a face that he hoped said *I'd love to give you a homeless dollar but the doors are welded shut and the windows don't roll up or down.*

The homeless guy waved and smiled back and started walking to the Ciera and waved through the rolled-up passenger window. The Ciera only moved about 3 feet and was parked again so Lenny slammed the car into park. He rolled down his drivers' window and then took off his seatbelt so he could stick his head out the window and tell the homeless guy about the passenger side of the Ciera.

The homeless guy was like Lenny in that he didn't hear so good. Lenny picked up on it - and waved him over to the drivers' side while displaying a homeless dollar in his waving hand.

"Ain't it a beautiful night out?"

is what the homeless guy said to Lenny.

"Not if the Gatorade bottle is full."

Lenny said.

The homeless guy looked in and saw the Gatorade bottle and did the math.

"You need to go pee?"

"About a half hour ago…"

The homeless guy took the dollar and said

"Well I know lots of good places to go pee and you don't need a Gatorade bottle or anything. But you probably do need to get offa this street here."

Just then the cars were moving another three feet, and the guy in the pickup truck behind Lenny was honking his horn and yelling for him to move it. Lenny wondered what the big hurry was to move three feet. But another car started honking, and then another and Lenny had to go pee and was frustrated. So, Lenny put the car in gear and moved three feet and when he did he ran over the homeless guy's left foot. He stopped when he heard the homeless guy yell but all that did was stop the Ciera right smack on the homeless guy's foot.

"AGHHHRRRHRHRHROWWWWW!!"

the homeless guy screamed.

"Oh god oh god. I'm sorry."

Lenny said.

"CAN YOU MOVE THE CAR OFFA MY FOOT!!??"

Lenny inched forward and felt the crunching of the homeless guy's foot before he rolled the tire to the safety of the pavement.

Lenny said

"Get in the back seat."

The homeless guy limped a step and opened the door and fell into the car.

"This is quite a nice car sir. I really like velour."

The homeless guy said.

Lenny didn't want to talk about the Ciera or the velour or anything else until he found the place to go pee.

"OK – I'm really sorry about your foot – and I don't mean to be rude or anything – but where can I go pee without the Gatorade bottle?"

"Just turn up into that parking lot up there by the statue and I'll show you a fine place to go pee."

The homeless guy said.

Maybe the statue was 20 yards away but it looked like 20 miles. Every couple of minutes the Ciera moved three feet, and Lenny was putting both feet on the brake pedal really hard and was bouncing on the seat.

"Hang on there, sir – it's only a few minutes."

Said the homeless guy who had no appreciation for what it was like for Lenny when he had to go pee.

In just about the nick of time the Ciera got to where Lenny could turn into the parking lot.

"WHERE? WHERE? WHERE?"

Lenny screamed as he jetted between posts and cars.

"Sir you just go around the back over there behind those posts you'll see a dumpster. Might even be some toilet paper still there I stashed a while back."

The homeless guy said.

"I ain't gonna make it…"

Lenny said.

And he stopped the car in the middle of the parking lot and jumped out. He unzipped his shorts and pulled his pecker out and went right there in the open.

In Lenny's life, there had been several moments that gave him pause that he knew would stay with him forever. And as the warm urine hit the hot pavement and he felt such intense relief almost like an orgasm he knew that this would be one of those.

And after the first little bit where he still had to strain and grunt it turned out to be about the best pee he ever had. Even though the pickup truck was going the same place he was and was right behind the Ciera and the guy was honking the horn and yelling the whole time. How come it always happened that the car you just don't wanna be around seems to always be around you?

After the pee and the apology to the pickup truck guy Lenny got back in the Ciera and parked in a parking space.

"Whew. OOOOHHHH. Ahhhhh. Man."

Lenny said looking straight out the windshield.

"You feel better now sir?"

The homeless guy said while he laughed in the backseat.

"Yeah…"

Lenny said.

"Sir I'm Patch and it's nice to meet you."

"Oh."

Lenny turned around and extended his hand to Patch who was laying down on the velour.

"I used to be Lenny Franks."

"Who are you now?"

"I don't know. That's a good question. Call me Lenny I guess."

"Hi Lenny."

Patch kept talking about what a beautiful night it was and how he felt so lucky to be alive when it was this beautiful outside. He also said what a fine car the Ciera was, and how comfortable the velour seat was, and thanks again for the homeless dollar only he just called it a dollar.

Patch puzzled Lenny even though he didn't know anything about Patch.

"How's your foot?"

Lenny asked.

"Oh, it'll be fine Lenny just fine."

Patch was a black homeless man. Lenny knew a few black humans but not too many. This might have been the first black homeless man he knew though and he had some questions for Patch. Here are the questions Lenny asked Patch in the order he asked them:

"Your sign says homeless so are you homeless?

Do you live in Las Vegas?

Where are you from?

Do you have any family?

Did you ever wear a mouth guard for sleeping?

Where do you eat?

Is there a God?

Do you have a cellphone for emergencies?

How much money do you make?"

And here are the answers Patch gave in order.

"I don't have a house but the world is my home and it's the best world we got and it's a damned fine place to live you better believe that. I just use the sign because it's easier for folks to understand. For now, I'm in Las Vegas but the world is my home and it's the best world we got you better believe that. I'm from Earth.

Oh, I got a sister and a son and he got a little family and friends and now that we're friends I got one more and that's a damned fine thing to happen on such a beautiful night. I don't know what that means.

Here and there. Tops of trash cans have the best stuff in the world. You can't believe what people throw away here. Had a great burger from *IN N OUT* for dinner tonight, right up the road.

Oh yes there's a God and he made the best world we got and so I thank him every day for that.

No, I don't because Lenny because I believe these cellphones will be the end of us except sometimes when I got the money I buy emergency cellphones.

Not much but I don't need much because God has made the best world we got."

Lenny was really happy about the cellphone answer but pretty confused about the rest of it. How could Patch who slept outside, and went pee in parking lots near light posts, and ate food out of trash cans, believe in God and be this happy and think this was a beautiful world and a beautiful night? And the weirdest one – this is the best world we got?

So, Lenny decided to feel sorry for Patch and thought about saving him too and said

"Patch I'm glad we're friends but don't you ever look around and see how shitty the world is? I mean how can banks get away with it? And how about the cellphone companies and the doctors and the dentists and the stores that are always trying to add fees on? And how about the small print? And how about how bosses and jobs? And how confusing it is just to buy peanut butte? And how come the apartment building people don't wanna fix your air conditioning? And why do people keep wanting to take pieces from you all the time?"

"You lookin at all the wrong stuff Lenny." Patch said with a busted-up foot but a huge smile on his face.

And right then Lenny Franks decided that he was sure Patch was somebody he needed to spend more time with. Truthfully – Lenny didn't need to save Patch and he would come to figure that out. In fact, and wouldn't ya know it but it would be Patch who would ultimately play a huge role in Saving Lenny Franks.

CHAPTER 16

Patch was still sitting in the back of the Ciera and smiling while he was rubbing his right hand on the velour. Lenny turned around again, and asked Patch where the best fancy hotel was that wasn't too expensive to take a shower and sleep on a bed. It had been too long and Lenny was all Americanized and so on. Patch said he had no earthly idea. He said he had never been in one of those fancy hotel rooms and that he hadn't had a shower in about a month. Lenny finally figured out what it was that he smelled.

"Is your foot ok Patch?"

Lenny asked.

"Oh, it's fine Lenny, fine. Don't worry so much about it. If I could just rest for a little while I would be awfully appreciative."

Patch said.

Lenny said sure. But he was thinking about that fancy hotel room and clean bed and shower. And he was feeling guilty about running over Patch's foot. He couldn't just leave him here. But he couldn't take him with him to the fancy hotel either.

Then Lenny looked at the tattoo on his arm and even though it didn't have the s at the end of opinion he figured this was the way he meant to live his new life. It couldn't just be words on his arm.

"Patch, I was really looking forward to that fancy hotel room. It's been a while. And well – I feel responsible for your foot and all and – well – maybe you'd like to stay with me for the night in the fancy hotel?"

Lenny said.

"Oh, that's awful nice of you Lenny. But I be fine right here on the velour, if that's ok with you."

Patch said.

Lenny was relieved. And he knew how to make it even better for Patch.

"OK Patch – I have the blanket my grandma made in the trunk that you can use, and actually I could use somebody to keep an eye on Teddy while I go to the hotel."

"Who's Teddy?"

Lenny told Patch about Teddy as he got the blanket from the trunk and helped Patch get all set up. He gave Teddy to Patch and took the water bottle out of his backpack too and set it next to his new friend.

"Patch – I'm just going to go across the street to Bugsy Segal's joint – The Flamingo. It's the first one on the strip really. I stayed there a few times during the war actually."

Lenny said.

Patch let that one go and pulled the blanket up even tighter.

"OK Lenny, have a good night. Me and Teddy be right here when you get back."

"Thanks Patch."

"Lenny – you see – ain't this a beautiful night? Ain't this about the best world we got?"

Lenny looked down at Patch through the window and said,

"I'll let ya know after the shower."

And then he turned and walked toward the Flamingo.

CHAPTER 17

What he remembered about Las Vegas was that you could cross the busy street that went right down the middle anywhere you wanted if there weren't any cars coming. But as Lenny looked at the cars still stopped along the glittering Las Vegas Boulevard he saw that there were fences up everywhere, and nowhere to cross. He looked around and spotted enormous overpasses and humans walking over them to cross the street. Lenny shook his head and thought to himself that this had to be just another way they were trying to screw him.

It wasn't easy to figure it all out and there were lots and lots of new humans to negotiate, but the lights were on full blast and there were so many breasts to look at that Lenny got distracted enough. He got lost at the end and wound up where you got the taxicabs. He saw people with suitcases lined up to the top of the escalator. They were waiting in line for their rooms and they all looked miserable. And every single one of them had their cellphones out and their heads down.

He had come this far and so he was going to sleep in a real bed and have a shower and that was the end of it. But standing in that line got him thinking about the world again. How could they not have enough humans behind the counter? How come none of them to give a flying fuck? Why was it like this? Everywhere? All the time? Was this really the best world we got?

It was about 35 minutes later that Lenny got to the front of the line. Of course, just then two of the people behind the counter just left so he had to wait even more. Finally, it was his turn and he went up to one of the counters where there was a young guy who didn't even say hi or welcome to the Flamingo or even can I help you.

So, Lenny jumped in.

"Hello – I used to be Lenny Franks and she broke up with me but we're back together now I think and with everything going on I'm headed to Los Angeles and Patch wanted to sleep on the velour in the Ciera with Teddy and so it's just me. I need a room with a nice bed and a shower please."

"Do you have a reservation?"

The young guy behind the counter said with his head down.

"No."

said Lenny.

The young guy behind the counter shook his head and said

"Hmmmm that's a problem."

"I figured."

There was no way for Lenny to know, being that the young guy wasn't wearing a name badge, but Lenny had found his way to the milieu of one Travis Miller, a recent USC graduate with a BA in Economics and the proud owner of student loans totaling over a quarter of a million dollars. That was another way they got ya. Put a young guy or a girl in debt so deep they had to take shitty jobs just to pay off the debt. That's how it was for Travis Miller.

So, this is a story about Travis and his mother that you don't really have to read unless you like the other stories and think this one might be worth hearing about. It's totally up to you.

Young Travis or *Travie Dear* as his mother *Michellene* called her only son had been working at the hotel for only a few months and he hated it. He pretty much hated everything about his life and he had come to the hating quite honestly.

Travis Sr. was killed in a recreational boating accident involving a twisted nylon anchor rope, the propeller of a 125-horsepower Mercury outboard engine, and a mixture of hydrocodone tablets and cheap rum. The insurance company refused to pay out citing that since it was 3:00 am on a Tuesday morning when the accident occurred, and that Travis Miller, Sr. was alone and blasted on the lake on a friend's boat that he had "borrowed", without permission. Further, the insurance company declared, the pilot of the craft appeared to have exercised extremely poor judgment all the way round, and so it was hardly the responsibility of *The Mutual Insurance Company of Central Iowa* to make remittance. The final toxicology report ended any thought his widow had about pressing the matter.

Michellene was not the widow Miller's given name of course. Michelle Schwartz-Miller had changed her name after the boating accident. She and 6-year-old Travis then relocated to Southern California where she found work as an exotic dancer. At *Jiggles West*, she regularly performed a trick with ping pong balls and a Velcro dartboard that never failed to impress or attract big tips.

She was then, with this income and the love and financial support of a stable of rotating older male friends, able to put a roof over *Travie Dear's* head and send him to the finest public elementary and high schools the greater Inglewood area could provide. Travis did most of his homework and played intramural squash and even found time to be in the schools' macramé club. His grades were respectable and USC accepted him but offered little financial aid.

Travis had dreams of escaping and doing big things with his life but nobody at USC thought to mention that his Economics degree would be useful only if he were to follow it up with more schooling or know someone (and he knew no one) in the field or have a desire to teach mathematics in the Inglewood school district.

Michellene who was then in her 40's, found new life in the adult online chatroom business and relocated to Las Vegas a year earlier. She was able to rent a modest home with a guest room. With very few options *Travie Dear* followed his mother to Las Vegas and applied for work in the always bustling hospitality business there. She moved the computer with the chat room camera out of the guest room and into her own room. He was turned down several times before the Flamingo offered him a job. His salary just about covered his monthly expenses including the student loan payments and a room and board stipend to his mother, but the job offered little other than the frustration of dealing with tourists looking for cheap lodging and free booze. He had no incentives other than to show up and stand there and so that's what he did and not very well. His boss frequently reminded him that the company was having financial troubles and that if he didn't like working there that there would be 100 people waiting to work there for even less money.

After *Travie Dear* with his head still down pushed about 50 buttons on Lenny's behalf he said

"Ok we have one room but it's a junior executive state room with a living area. There's no strip view and it's two queens. It's $795.00."

Back in the day, when he was still Lenny Franks, he would have thought the same thing he was thinking now but he would have taken the room. But now 795 bucks was a TON of money.

"Nothing else?"

Lenny asked.

"Just bigger rooms for more money."

What happened to there being just one room...

"OK – I'll just go sleep in the Ciera with Patch and Teddy then."

Travis looked at his watch as Lenny walked away. Forty more minutes and he could go home and go to his guest room and masturbate to pornography and fall asleep.

On his way to the escalator Lenny could hear the racket from the Casino so he cautiously moved that way. He could win money. Why not? Somebody had to. Pay for the room and maybe add to the pot. He had the few thousand dollars Lenny, Sr. had given him that was accounted for on the ledger, and that would get him along for at least a few months if he was careful. He thought Las Vegas owed him for Chrissakes. He had given them enough money during the war.

He walked up to one of the machines with cartoons on it and looked for the slot where you put the coins. He'd be damned but there wasn't one. Not on any of the machines. He looked for the change booth to ask what the hell was going on and he couldn't find a change booth or a Change Girl.

Lenny saw that you could put actual dollars in a slot on each of the machines. So, he pulled out his wallet and took out a Ten. The machine burped it back the first time, but he tried it again and it begrudgingly accepted his offering.

"BARRRINGGG" the machine belched.

He looked for a handle to pull or even a button to push or what the hell to do but he got all flustered. There were all these options and buttons and blinking lights.

"PLAY THE MAX!"

a cartoon voice screeched.

Lenny almost had a heart attack until he figured out the cartoon voice was coming from inside the machine. He got so frustrated looking at this button and that and he was tired from the day and he had to go pee again so he just looked for the coin return button. There wasn't one.

Oh god… Lenny thought.

Well – it's only 10 bucks and not 795 – and – you're first loss is your least loss is what Lenny Franks, Sr. always said, so Lenny left the machine and started back toward the escalator with a stop at the bathroom.

Which meant he didn't see the woman who was sitting a couple machines down who noticed that he left some credits in the machine slide over to Lenny's machine and push one button and hit for $ 2,500.00. It was perfect timing for her. She hadn't found any dates that night and had just come off her leanest month in her new job as a chatroom artist.

Maybe she'd take her son *"Travie Dear"* out for dinner after his shift.

But probably not.

CHAPTER 18

Here's a few things you don't know about Lenny Franks, and a few things you do or might have guessed about, just to make sure everybody's on the same page.

He used to be married for a long time. He liked being married mostly but a lot of the time he felt like he was just the guy who paid for everything. He and his wife got along fine but slept in different rooms most nights and were having fewer and fewer orgasms together with each passing year. They were friends and after a while they both thought that they could still be friends and Lenny could still pay for everything even if they slept in different rooms in different houses so that's what they did.

After he finished up with that marriage Lenny Franks had no interest in being married again. His Ex-wife was still his friend and they talked all the time and he figured if he wanted to have an orgasm with a woman well he could find somebody to do that with. He met a few new ones and had a few orgasms, and they seemed to like him and they all even wanted to be married again. But Lenny already did that and didn't want to wind up being the guy who just paid for everything and slept in a different room and saw his orgasms dwindle all over again. So, he left or they left and it never caused him a minute's distress.

He was loose and cool and walked around like he had the world by the balls most of the time because he did, and then he met his new girlfriend. She was young and pretty and smart. She thought Lenny was funny and crazy and loose and cool and they hit it off right away. He doesn't talk about orgasms with her because it's nobody's business. Let's just say this one was different for Lenny. He still had some good jobs and things going on and they had fun together. She was so much younger than he was, and that was part of the fun, and also it meant that there was no chance in hell they were gonna fall in love or anything. And like him she hated cell phones which was weird for somebody that much younger. But boy did she ever. She could never remember where she put it. He never asked her if she saw the Aliens in her head or anything but he did wonder about it. He really loved her and he wanted to save her and be with her.

They fell in love sonofagun, and at the time they were getting deeper in it Lenny started to have fewer good jobs and less fun stuff going on. It pecked away at him and he wasn't as loose and cool and well – he wasn't like the old Lenny Franks or even the Lenny Franks she met and fell in love with. She didn't want him to save her and she couldn't figure out how to save him. He would look at his cellphone all the time to see if she called or sent him messages. He wondered where she was all the time. She had this young life and he had this old life and not the life he thought he was going to have. Oh, she wasn't perfect either of course and that's kinda the point though. She had her shit and he had his and he knew enough to know that if you're in you're in, and you hang in there and tolerate each other's shit. She didn't know about this yet. And to be fair Lenny was a handful for anybody, and with Lenny being not so much like the old Lenny or even the new Lenny it got hard for her. One day he thought he should leave, and the next day she thought she should, and they bounced around with that for a while. Until one day she finally really left and for days he would look at his phone and wish hard to see her name. He would cry even though he never really cried, except sometimes at movies. He missed her so terribly. And when the phone finally did ring and he had that talk with her, he was happy but scared. He wanted her to be with him but wondered if it might happen again. If he might get crazy or she might get scared.

Funny thing though that on the drive to Los Angeles, and now with meeting Patch, getting the tattoo, and looking out the windows and telling himself all the time not to worry about what was gonna happen next, he didn't seem to look at his cellphone so much. Oh, he missed her and wished she was there with him but he started feeling better about the whole thing and thought about more things than just her all the time.

It was like Lenny Franks was becoming Lenny Franks again except maybe another different version of Lenny Franks. He thought a lot about how not everybody saw things the way he did, and that's what made the whole thing sorta wonderful if he wanted to look at it that way. With a lot of the trash out of his head about what everybody else thought of him, he was making progress. He didn't have to save everybody and that was starting to find its way in there too. He had to let Patch sleep in the car because he ran over his foot but maybe he didn't have to fix the guy's whole life. He knew there would be more pain and bullshit because life is full of pain and bullshit. He knew that she might throw him for a loop again and he hoped not but that's also what happens sometimes. He had to be ok no matter what. That's hard to do, but he was at least now thinking that somehow and someway with what was already in there with the old Lenny Franks, and what was starting to bubble with the new Lenny Franks, and that maybe just maybe there was a way through all of this. So what if he didn't have a job or a lot of money or didn't know what he was doing or where he was living and he couldn't be in the same room with her and the only time he could talk to her was every few days on the phone? So what?

He was still Lenny Fucking Franks and when he remembered that and got his brain around it all things were possible.

Chapter 19

When the sun came up the next morning, Patch was still sleeping like a baby with the blanket draped on him and his head resting nicely on the velour in the back seat of the Ciera. He had Teddy clutched to his chest, and he was smiling. But Lenny was another story.

The Ciera was the kind with two seats in the front and a middle compartment for homeless dollars, instead of how the back seat went all the way across for sleeping. After he found his way back from the Flamingo, which wasn't as easy as you'd think because nothing ever is, he climbed over to the passenger side seat. There's more room on the side without the steering wheel, and he tried to lean the seat back as far as it could go. It didn't go back at all. Lenny put his feet on the dashboard and pushed with all his might but the seat didn't move. He screamed at God but that didn't work because he didn't believe in God and he didn't think God cared about things like car seats or football games or wars anyway. The screaming also did not wake up Patch.

Patch had the blanket and Teddy and Lenny had nothing but his light jacket. And sitting upright got old fast. Also, the smell inside the Ciera from Patch was making Lenny feel like he wanted to vomit.

It was like somebody bagged up a bunch of rotten eggs and threw a dead goat and some used motor oil in there and tossed it all on the back seat of the Ciera and then took a dump on top of it just for good measure before they left.

Lenny knew he couldn't stay inside the car, and so he went outside and looked around for options and settled on trying to sleep on his hood. He might have dozed off a couple times for a few minutes each but who can say for sure.

When the sun came up he thought he should probably get on with it and get off the hood which turned out to be a bit of a problem. Lenny had been in a car wreck some years earlier, where he broke his back. Lying on a cold metal hood for the better part of four hours wasn't ideal. He eventually mustered the energy to roll over onto his side and slide off the hood and onto his feet, but he was bent over when he landed and he stayed that way for a little while.

Once he got himself standing up nearly fully erect but in considerable pain, he looked inside the car and saw Patch laying on his back with his eyes open but he looked dead. Lenny went to the back-passenger door that opened and he opened it. Patch still didn't move.

Lenny said

"Hey Patch Hey Patch! Hey Patch!"

Patch finally blinked and looked at Lenny.

"Oh, and a good morning to you Lenny Franks! All rested up after your night in the fancy hotel and a good shower! But I'll tell you what Lenny – I don't know that you could beat how comfortable I slept last night on this here velour. It might be the best night sleep I've had in my entire life!"

That sounded about right. The world was a silly place.

CHAPTER 20

Sal1111, the chief *Banglordian* Software programmer and engineer
had his own cabin inside *BL-001,* that served as both his office and
sleeping and eating quarters. He was one of the few to have space like
this inside the big ship, but it was necessary and he worked best this way.
He was a cluster of one and that's how it had to be. The rest of the ship
had mostly wide-open spaces with no beams inside, so all the
Banglordian clusters could roam and sleep together when they needed to.
There were other large rooms where the saltwater was kept in large bins
with multiple spouts and dispensers for plastic and rubber and sticks. But
for *1111,* there were small custom saltwater bins and food dispensers
inside his cabin.

He spent his days looking at screens tracking the demise of the
humans on earth and eating and sleeping when he had to. He learned
their language in minutes, and found how easy it was to push their
buttons with literally, the push of a few buttons. The screens kept him
laughing all the time, and so there were lots of tiny cubes all over the
place, but the cabin also had its own system for cube collection and
disposal. *Sal1111* was self-sufficient and in fact operated best without

distraction. Every now and then *Banglordians* got one like that and they put him to good use.

When he started way back when with the first insertion of the *SNS1022* chips, he had an idea of what might happen but humans quickly exceeded his wildest expectations. He came to the conclusion very early that this was a species that to a man or woman was almost always acting in their own self-interest with little regard for how anyone or anything else would be affected. They were rushing, always rushing, from one thing to the next and doing many things at the same time, and of course this meant they were doing none of it very well at all. In fact, it looked to him like they were having contests to see who could pile on the most shit and be the busiest. They bragged to each other about how much shit they piled up in their own brains and lives. They wasted incalculable amounts of time on the most trivial. They were overwhelmingly stressed out and obnoxiously afraid of all the wrong stuff and didn't laugh nearly enough.

The technology insertion worked like gasoline on a small brush fire in a very dry wood. Humans became even more self-centered and isolated and busy and afraid. And *1111* with a push of a button could accelerate the pace. He would type a suggestion into the translator and through sophisticated *Banglordian* algorithmic programs humans would see images and messages on their tiny screens and all hell would break loose. The basic psychology of primitive stupid races meant they were so easy to train. Like the dogs with the bells. With a BING or a SWOOSH or a BA-DING, humans would stop everything and snap to it and give their gadgets their full attention. They would stop conversations and look away from loved ones and take their eyes off the road. He made sure they stayed distracted and confused and afraid and had things to blow each other up with. It wasn't all that hard given what he had to work with down there.

Today was a big day, because although the humans were certainly on their way, the *Banglordians* were getting closer to the rendezvous time of the two ships and the final stretch run to their new home. Humans were disappearing at a good rate but needed some more little pushes. Some large clusters of humans were talking about firing things to blow up other large clusters of humans and that could be very useful. Humans were so easy to nudge along. And what a gift to *Banglordia* was this guy in the most powerful human cluster who was so easy to wind up and set off. It was like they had their own guy down there, only their own guy couldn't be this helpful. So *Sal1111* pushed a few buttons and messages appeared on tiny screens on earth, and everybody stopped whatever they were doing and their heads snapped, and the next thing you know humans in that most powerful cluster jumped right in. Enough of them agreed that blowing up another cluster was a good idea. Had to show we mean business and so on. The primitive radioactive waste and fallout was no problem for *Banglordians,* and in fact contained properties for healthier *Banglordian* teeth.

1111 was a little sad that this unending laugh fest of watching humans go a few at a time by the silliest ways of driving into each other while looking at their tiny screens, shooting each other by the dozens or hundreds, or by finally lining up for collection at the technology stores would take too long because he could have watched that stuff and laughed and shat cubes for the rest of his life. But they needed the planet so that was that. Humans would not be able to take their eyes of their screens, and no power on earth could make them take their eyes of their screens, and so it was just a matter of time until it all came together. That was the key to the whole thing. And the *Banglordians* had very willing partners with these humans.

Just a few more weeks now and *Sal1111* and the rest would be on their new home and the few remaining humans would be gathered up and put on *BL-001* and *BL-002* and set adrift into space, where they would in all likelihood tear each other to pieces in a matter of weeks.

Chapter 21

Lenny told Patch about the problems at the Flamingo and how he had to sleep in the car. He left out the part about sleeping on the hood because of the smell. Patch said he was sorry about that but he knew a place where they could both get a shower and clean their clothes if Lenny had some quarters. Lenny thought that was a very good idea.

Lenny started driving and Patch stayed in the back seat but was now sitting up. He smiled the whole way as he was directing Lenny to the shower place.

"Oh Lenny, ain't this a beautiful day?"

Patch said while looking out the window.

"Oh yeah...."

Lenny said.

"Lenny, I love this time of day. The world just gettin goin and all the people gettin their days started. There's so many things can happen in a day and it's all just startin now. You ever heard this one that the afternoon knows what the mornin never even thought about?"

"Hmmm."

Patch led Lenny to a do it yourself car wash and motioned for him to go into the far stall. Lenny thought the Ciera needed a bath too so he didn't mind the stop.

"OK Patch – we'll wash the car first then and go to the shower place."

Lenny said.

Patch laughed.

"Lenny – this IS the shower place!"

"You gotta be shitting me."

Lenny said.

"Oh no they work really good but it's a two-man job. You just gotta be careful because the water comes out like bullets, so you gotta squeeze the trigger just a little bit but you'll get the hang of it."

Patch said.

"What the hell?"

Lenny said but pulled the Ciera into the garage furthest away from the street. He centered it, and shut the car off and grabbed his backpack and put Teddy inside and got out of the car. Patch worked himself over to the door and limped out to join Lenny at the box where you put the quarters in.

"OK Lenny, put them quarters in there and let's do the car first then so you can get the hang of the water gun."

Patch said.

Lenny took the quarters from the change compartment in the backpack and started forcing them into the slot on the box. The light turned green and the water WHOOOSHED and Lenny put the backpack out of harms' way and picked up the water gun.

"OK now – just squeeze it a little like you're tickling it."

Patch said.

"I know how to work a water gun Patch"

Lenny said.

The lack of sleep and the pain in his lower back and the lack of food and the absurdity of the operation started to get to Lenny.

"OK Lenny you're a pro – go ahead."

Lenny out of sheer frustration squeezed the trigger as hard as he could and blasted the water across the hood of the Ciera. Patch stayed quiet.

Lenny kept peppering the Ciera with short and long bursts from the water gun and actually experienced a much-needed cathartic release. Sort of like an orgasm. It was not Lenny's first rodeo and he deftly re-holstered the water gun and grabbed the soapy brush and vigorously cleaned the Ciera. Lenny had to brush extra hard on the front bumper and windshield to get the dead bugs to come loose. He followed all that up with another series of bursts from the water gun until the Ciera was as clean as it had been in days.

The Ciera gleamed and dripped beaded water. Lenny inserted more quarters in the slot, and looked at Patch with a fresher set of eyes and a sudden surge of energy. While he went about the business of rolling down the two windows that actually rolled down in an attempt to fumigate the interior, he turned his attention to Patch.

"Patch – let's get you cleaned up."

Lenny said.

Regarding Patch in full it struck him that this would be more of an operation than he initially thought.

"Tell ya what – why don't I give you my extra T-shirt and pair of shorts and we'll hose your clothes down and let them dry out a bit."

Lenny said.

Patch was almost moved to tears by the gesture he mistook for the purest form of kindness. In truth, Lenny wasn't going to let Patch back into the Ciera with those clothes regardless of whether they had washed them out or not.

"Lenny – that's about the nicest thing anybody done for me in a long time…"

Patch managed.

"It's the least I can do."

Lenny said and he meant it. He always thought that was a funny thing to say because in truth he believed it meant that could he have done any less – that's what he would have done.

Patch stripped naked and set his dirty and foul-smelling clothes on the ground next to the Ciera. If it was possible, Patch's clothes looked even more disgusting laying on the ground. Lenny didn't want those clothes washed out or not anywhere near the Ciera. He took a long look at them and said to Patch

"Hey man – why don't we just throw those in the trash? You can keep the ones I'm giving you till we figure out what to do."

Naked Patch said

"Oh Lenny – you might be a saint you know that?"

"Saint Lenny, Yep."

Lenny said taking the water gun in his right hand and jerking the trigger in small test bursts next to Patch.

"Ready Patch?"

"Oh, I sure am Lenny – I haven't had a shower in weeks."

Patch said. It was information Lenny was already sure he had.

Naked Patch said

"Let's try my back first."

and then he turned and put his hands on the hood of the Ciera and spread his legs. Lenny assumed that wasn't the first time Patch had been in that exact position and then asked himself if that might be a racist thing to think.

"Hey Patch, you ever had the cops ask you to spread em?"

"Not for a long time Lenny."

Lenny decided the whole mental excursion and subsequent exercise got him no further on the matter. He squeezed the trigger like he practiced and got the hang of it really quick. He sprayed water all over naked Patch who screamed a little because the water was cold, but it also seemed to Lenny that Patch was enjoying it. Lenny went to the box and hit the button so the soap would come out. He shot soapy water on Patch then returned the button to the rinse position to finish the shower.

Lenny was careful when it came to shooting the water and the soap on Patch's front side near his nuts and his pecker. Even with the cold-water, Lenny was impressed by the size of Patch's pecker. Lenny had been told over the years that he himself had a good-sized pecker, but if he was truthful about it he was no match for Patch.

Patch spread his arms in the air and said

"Oh, Lenny thank you for this wonderful shower. After I dry off I'll put on clean clothes and I'll be good as new. Except for my foot but sometimes you need something not so good to remind you about all the good stuff."

Lenny was getting tired of Patch sounding like a self-help book all the time.

"Lenny – you about the best shower giver since Wrigley."

Patch said.

"Wrigley?"

Lenny said.

"Oh – Wrigley a friend of mine – only I ain't seen him in a while. He's from Chicago but I don't know where he off to these days."

Patch said.

"So, he was named after Wrigley Field?"

Lenny asked?

"Oh no – the chewin gum."

Patch responded.

"Same thing."

Lenny said.

"I don't know about that."

Patch said.

With Patch air drying Lenny walked to the backpack and fished out the T-shirt and the other pair of shorts and walked them over to Patch.

"Here you go…"

Lenny said. He was actually kind of proud of himself for taking care of Patch. But he was careful about not wanting to get in it up to his ass and rescue him. The new Lenny Franks wasn't in the rescuing business anymore. But he could be in the car wash showering business he decided.

Patch got dressed and only fell once on account of his busted foot but he laughed and stayed in good humor. He went for his old beat up shoes and Lenny decided this would have to be addressed as well.

"Patch – I got a pair of flip flops in here – why don't you see if they fit."

"Lenny, you about the kindest man I ever met."

Patch said.

"Then that's a shame."

Lenny said under his breath.

Patch put on the flip flops and limped around by the car. He was smiling ear to ear as he looked over his new wardrobe. Lenny thought he actually saw a tear under Patch's right eye, but it could have just been water from the car wash shower that hadn't dried up yet.

"OK Lenny – your turn for the shower!"

Patch said.

Lenny stripped and assumed the position on the hood of the Ciera and waited for Patch to hit him with the water.

"Jesus Christ!!! Jesus Christ!!!!"

Lenny shrieked after getting hit with the first sprays of the cold water. After a few seconds, he was enjoying it. It felt good and it woke him up in a most pleasing way. Lenny was laughing.

Maybe Patch was onto something. These little things that he's taken for granted like a shower, or clean clothes, or velour seats…

"It's good to laugh ain't it Lenny? I mean if we got the choice – and we always got the choice – wouldn't you rather be laughing."

Lenny laughed and considered this as he ran the soap through his hair and closed his eyes and felt the water wash down his body. Patch was laughing and Lenny was smiling and in that instant, the world at this moment was indeed a pretty good place Lenny thought. He didn't even think about what was gonna happen next.

What did happen a split second later a soul jarring shriek and a cannon blast to the crotch.

And for a brief instant the only thing that Lenny registered was that Patch had just shot him in the pecker in front of a screaming little girl.

CHAPTER 22

Here's how crazy the world is and how things just sorta come together at the weirdest times. These are just the arbitrary things that happen to humans on earth through no fault of their own. They didn't just happen to Lenny. They happened to everybody. This is a story about exactly that.

Rosa Alvarez was 13 years-old and loved Saturday mornings. As the youngest of four girls, it was one of the rare times she had her father's complete attention. Her three older sisters, Maria, Anna and stepsister Gretchen, all slept in till after noon on weekends, which was a function of both their ages and the need to recuperate following the previous evenings' shenanigans.

Anthony *Big Belly* Alvarez also looked forward to the weekends and the time he would spend with Rosa. The other three were already lost causes. They drank and smoked weed and worked menial jobs and *Big Belly* was pretty sure were all very morally corruptible and in fact were already morally corrupt.

The love of his life Angelina had passed a few years earlier right at the time Maria and Anna needed their mother the most. *Big Belly* was immediately overwhelmed and latched onto the first promising maternal replacement he found. He got into it too fast and it was already too late because Helga and her teenage daughter Gretchen served only to accelerate his elder daughters' demises. Most troubles in life come from saying yes to quickly or no not soon enough, *Big Belly's* father used to say to him.

Helga did a fine job during the courtship of concealing both her own methamphetamine addiction and Gretchen's juvenile record. When the families merged it was an immediate and unmitigated disaster.

But Rosa would not go down this path, and on this point *Big Belly* was adamant. No matter what it took, or how much it cost him, he would protect his little Rosa. He bought her a cellphone and was in contact with her several times daily. He would meet her at school for lunch twice weekly and more on the days his painting job had him in the neighborhood. He went to every dance recital and school event and started a small college fund for her. This was his last and best chance at redemption. There was never enough time or money but *Big Belly* would find a way.

"Papa, Papa! Can we go to the carwash today?"

Little Rosa asked.

"Of course, baby. Then, we'll go get breakfast and we'll go hiking."

Big Belly said.

Rosa loved going to the carwash. Her Dad let her put the coins in the machine and run the operation. She was the boss at the carwash.

"Papa, get the hose…"

"Papa, get the towels…"

"Papa you missed a spot…"

Big Belly took Rosa's hand and led her to his truck, and opened the door for his princess, and kissed her on the forehead while she put on her seatbelt. He pulled out of the driveway and let Rosa pick the radio station as always and smiled while he enjoyed the only part of his life that was still pure and good.

"Papa, where should we go for breakfast?"

Rosa asked as the truck was coming up on the carwash.

"Anywhere you want baby."

Big Belly said.

"I think I want pancakes today. Maybe we can go to The Silly Goose?"

"The Silly Goose it is little Rosa."

She was such an angel he thought. And he was going to keep it that way.

The sun was shining brightly and the sky was stark blue and streaked with wisps of clouds. The mountains in the background behind the car wash stall framed a magnificent desert scene. The air was warm and a gentle breeze welcomed a smiling *Big Belly* and his happy daughter as they hopped out of the truck. Today would be a good day. After breakfast and the hike, maybe they'd do a little shopping and run some errands. Anything, *Big Belly* thought, to keep his little Rosa at his side and away from the others and out of that house.

Rosa had a handful of quarters she grabbed from the truck's ashtray and was at the box putting them in the slot. The quarters weren't going in like they usually did. The first one got stuck, and Rosa tried to push it through with the one behind it, but could make no progress.

"Papa – the box is broken! It won't take the quarters!"

146

Rosa said.

"Let me look at that a minute."

Big Belly said and he walked over to join Rosa and the operation.

"Hmmm – it's stuck for sure. What should we do Rosa?"

"You keep trying Papa, and I'll go to the stall next door and see if that box works."

Rosa said.

"OK boss."

Big Belly said.

Rosa always liked it when her Papa called her boss. She strutted proudly out of her stall and around the corner to the next. For a second she looked down to her left hand to fetch a quarter and put it in her right. When she entered the adjacent stall, and looked up with the quarter in her hand, her little eyes were unprepared for what she saw.

There was a car and two men. The black man had clothes on and was hosing down a naked white man next to the car. She froze as her eyes took in more than anyone, let alone a sweet 13-year-old girl should have to see, and screamed as loudly as she ever had, summoning *Big Belly* to her side in a nanosecond.

Big Belly arrived in time to see the naked white man with his hands around his pecker and balls, and the black man holding the hose with his head turned toward Rosa and *Big Belly* and the source of the scream.

"Jesus Christ what are you two doing??!!"

Big Belly shouted.

He covered little Rosa's eyes and moved her behind him.

"Good mornin' sir."

Patch said without skipping a beat.

"It sure is a fine and beautiful morning ain't it?"

Lenny looked absently at *Big Belly* and Rosa and was unaware that he was still rubbing his nuts.

"A beautiful... what the hell is going on here?"

Big Belly said.

"And YOU - get your hands off your ... your... private parts and put some damned clothes on. I'm calling the police."

Patch moved as quickly as he could, hopping on his one good foot, to get Lenny his clothes. After tossing Lenny his shorts he hopped toward *Big Belly* and Rosa with his arms in the air.

"I sure am sorry bout all this Sir. I'm Patch and that's Lenny Franks. We had a rough time is all and we got gasoline all over us from the gas station and we was just tryin to get it offa us. We didn't mean to upset you or your little girl there."

Patch said.

This seemed to settle *Big Belly* down a bit.

"It's OK honey it's OK. Why don't you go back to the truck?"

Big Belly said to Rosa.

"Papa I don't want to go without you."

Rosa said.

Big Belly got agitated again.

"Listen you two clowns you get him dressed and you get the hell out of here and I mean now!"

"Yessir. We'll do that right away. And you and your little girl have a beautiful day."

Patch said.

Big Belly grunted and took Rosa around the corner and back to the truck. He shook his head and couldn't imagine how a simple thing like going to the carwash could be so devastating to his little girl.

Big Belly then considered that no matter what you did and how hard you tried life could just get up on its hind legs and knock you off your ass. He also thought that the world was taking pieces away from him and that he was running out of them fast.

CHAPTER 23

Transmission from *RUFUS622* to *Banglordian High Counsel* on *BL-002*. Earth Date September 19, 2017.

"Ship approaching perimeter approach for outer orbit vector for new home planet STOP Estimate by your latest transmission and trajectories that rendezvous with BL-002 to take place in .0043 Microfledgers (approximately two earth weeks)to join us in outer orbit vector STOP Enjoying latest transmissions from new home planet STOP Large scale Nuclear Blasting seems imminent STOP Can you believe the guy in charge of the most powerful human cluster STOP I keep thinking he's one of ours STOP Ready to discuss plans for scout units to make preliminary trips to new home planet after rendezvous STOP Please advise if you make any more stops STOP Otherwise will see you at rendezvous STOP"

Chapter 24

Lenny and Patch and Teddy made their way to a parking lot a couple of blocks down and decompressed. Nobody said anything for a few minutes.

"Well Lenny, least it was yours she saw and not mine... that mighta really scared her..."

Patch said.

Lenny couldn't help but disgorge a chuckle.

"Patch my boy it's always something ain't it?"

Lenny said.

"Sure is Lenny. Sure is."

Patch said.

"How's your foot?"

Lenny said turning around to face Patch.

"It's fine Lenny. Just fine."

"Well Patch – I feel bad and all – what can I do? You need a doctor or anything."

"Nah. It'll be just fine."

They sat silent for a few more moments.

"Lenny – you could drop me back over by the strip. I best be gettin' my day started and all. See what more adventures there are to come today."

"OK. I can do that."

Lenny said.

"Actually – if you don't mind – you could just drop me out by the freeway. I was thinkin bout headed to Los Angeles to visit my son and my new grandbaby. People always headin to Los Angeles on that freeway and it's pretty easy to get a hitch. Specially now I'm all cleaned up and everything."

Patch said.

Lenny considered this. They had never spoken to each other about their plans. In truth, everything had happened so fast in the hours since they'd met, there hadn't been time. But Lenny considered now that maybe it would be good to have some company and Patch he decided, might be the right guy.

"Do you know how to get to Los Angeles?"

Lenny asked Patch.

"Sure. You go to the ocean and take a left."

Patch replied.

"You know anything about girlfriends?"

"As much as the next guy."

"What are your feelings about windmills?"

"What should they be?"

Lenny made the decision right there.

"Patch, I'm actually headed to Los Angeles. I don't know what I'm doing and where I'm goin but I'm trying to figure all that out. I got a deal for ya. I'll take you to LA with me and pay for all the gas and food and everything if you help me. Then I'll help see if we can find you your grandbaby."

Patch dropped his head and started to get emotional. He looked up at Lenny, who was turned around facing him and said

"Lenny, that's the best offer I ever had. I take you up on that. You see Lenny I believe all things happen for a reason and you and me got together for a reason. This is the best world we got and right now I can't think of a better one."

Lenny started the Ciera and put it in gear and headed toward the highway. It was all he could do not to share his feelings with Patch about all things happening for a reason. But he did see that this was one hell of good turn of fortune for a guy who hadn't had one of those in a very long time.

CHAPTER 25

Both windows on the drivers' side were all the way down for the
first part of the trip to Los Angeles. Either the stench had dissipated or
Lenny had grown accustomed to it.

Lenny shifted in his seat and shifted again. He struggled to keep
his focus and his eyes on the road. The night spent tossing on the hood of
the Ciera, and the escapades of the morning at the carwash, and Patch's
constant platitudes, and his own general fatigue from going this far were
finally settling in. He hadn't heard from her in a few days. He was
getting cranky and he needed a nap.

Patch lay in the backseat with his head against the rear drivers'
door and his battered foot cradled on the front passenger headrest.

"Ain't it a beautiful day?"

Patch said as he continued looking out the window at the passing
sunlit desert rock.

When Lenny Franks got cranky you didn't want to be anywhere
near him. Before the war his friends *The Ace* and *Loop* even had a name
for it – *Lenny Moods*. And after hearing Patch talking about how

beautiful this was and how beautiful that was and how everything happened for a reason, combined with his own exhaustion and chewing on her some more well a *Lenny Mood* was nigh. He had kept it all bottled up for a while.

Finally, Lenny snapped.

"Patch – you're homeless! You sleep on the street and eat out of garbage cans for Chrissakes."

Lenny began.

Patch just let him run.

"Not everything happens for a reason Patch! My friend *Joey Bags'* cat died in a toilet accident! What is the reason for that? How is that everything happens for a reason?

Lenny continued on citing all the terrible things in the world. He didn't know his new friend well enough yet to tell him about the Aliens and their plans.

Patch listened politely and waited for his new friend to get it all out and then in a calm and quiet tone responded.

"I don't know why awful stuff happens Lenny I surely don't. And I'm sorry about your friend and his cat that sounds terrible. To be true with ya – I wonder sometimes too. Enough crazy stuff happened to me to over the years. But – and this is the gospel truth – this is the best world we got Lenny. We need two legs to walk so we got two legs. We need eyes to see – so we got eyes. You need some place to put our glasses on your face – so we got noses. And some day Lenny just like your friend's poor cat we gonna fall in and that'll be that. And I'll be damned if I ain't gonna do the best I can with it till that day happens."

Lenny considered all of that.

Then Patch started again

"Lenny I'm gonna see my grandbaby and you're gonna figure your life out and we're gonna have an adventure together. And you better believe it ain't gonna go perfect. But like Wrigley always say – ain't no steak without cowshit."

And if you asked Lenny about it right then he would have said some of it actually made sense and that it was really hard to argue with that last part.

CHAPTER 26

Man oh man, what a nap Lenny had. He sprung awake about 4 hours after he had crashed, and approximately 4 hours and 10 seconds after he parked the car at a rest stop. For the first time in days he actually felt reasonable. His right foot was asleep and he had drool all over his shirt but these were small concessions.

He turned and looked at Teddy and said

"I'll tell you what Gif - that was some nap."

Then he remembered about Patch but when he turned around Patch wasn't in the car.

Since the first order of business after a nap or any kind of sleeping for Lenny was to go pee, he locked the Ciera and marched to the restroom while shaking his right foot all the way. When he got to the urinal he grunted and strained and put his hands up on the wall above the shitter where the door didn't lock.

He finished up the first pee and got to the business of washing his hands in the dirty sink. There was no soap or paper towel. There was a busted hand dryer. He wondered if anybody ever did the math on paper towel saved versus electricity expended on hand dryers – and were we really better off?

He wiped his hands on his shorts as he went outside and looked around for Patch. Lenny found him sitting on a rock and looking at the desert.

"Lenny – how was that nap?"

Patch asked.

"Top five ever maybe."

Lenny said. He liked it when something cracked one of his *Top 5 Lists,* especially because it didn't happen very much anymore.

Patch said

"Lenny just look at how beautiful it is here. Ain't it somethin Lenny?"

All Lenny saw was dirt and rocks and all

Lenny felt was dust and the hot sun but he didn't want to get into it all over again so he just said

"Yep."

"Lenny, you ready for the windmills?"

Patch asked.

It should be explained here about Lenny Franks and large windmills. It can be traced back some forty years when he vacationing with his mom. They had driven the very stretch that he was now about to approach and the sky was dark and the windmills were spinning and whining. He got so freaked out, he asked his mom to turn the car around.

"Oh Lenny – they can't hurt you – they're just windmills."

Monica Franks told her son.

"Mama – I don't want to look at them anymore! They're like huge monsters"

Lenny responded.

"Lenny, close your eyes, and I'll put on *Cat Stevens* and we'll sing *Peace Train*.

This they did but Lenny had to peek every so often. They got through it but Lenny was scarred for life.

After that trip, and to this very day, Lenny couldn't listen to *Cat Stevens*. If he heard any *Cat Stevens* song he'd quickly switch the station or leave the party. If *Peace Train* came on he couldn't sleep for 3 days. It helped, but only a little, that *Cat Stevens* changed his name to *Yusuf Islam* and stopped making music.

Patch could sense Lenny's apprehension and already was grasping the rhythms of his new friend. Patch was intuitive like that. So was Lenny's girl. There really were so few people who got Lenny Franks.

Patch stood up from his rock and moved slowly on his one good foot toward Lenny.

"Lenny whatever is between you and those windmills well I know it upsets you. But this is your new life Lenny. Ain't gonna be easy. And you've come already so far. And I'm here with ya. Ain't nothin gonna happen to you long as I'm with you. You believe me, don't you?"

Patch said.

"OK Patch. Thanks. What the fuck. Let's do it."

Lenny said.

It's hard to pinpoint the well from which Lenny's newfound confidence sprung. Maybe it was Patch being there. Maybe it was that his girl was still talking to him. Maybe it was being free from his job and his life. But he wasn't going to stop.

That is until he saw the cluster of towers in the distance and the memories started flooding back. Patch sensed this and started telling stories to distract Lenny. The tales were colorful and varied and Patch jumped from one to the next.

But here's all Lenny heard:

"Sewing machine…"

"Potatoes and foil make good pipes…"

"Wrigley's nipple…"

"Oh lord Jesus her finger was frozen solid …"

The closer the Ciera got to the windmills the more nervous Lenny got. His hands crushed the steering wheel making his knuckles white hot. Every muscle in his body tensed up and his breathing was erratic.

"Lenny – hang on there, my friend – I'm right here with ya."

Patch said.

"Shit Patch! Shit Patch! Shit Patch!"

Lenny yelled back.

"Lenny – maybe we sing a song while we do this – always helps me to sing a song when things ain't like I want em."

"NOOOOO! No singing! I ain't wrecking another song!"

Lenny shrieked.

Lenny wondered how come everybody thought singing was a good idea at times like this.

"OK – no singing then Lenny."

Patch said. Then thought of something.

"Lenny – you suppose Teddy is ok with the windmills and all?"

Lenny considered this as he glanced over at Teddy sitting atop the backpack with his seatbelt on.

"I don't know Patch. He looks ok…"

"Teddy got a lotta courage Lenny. But maybe if you freakin out he freaks out."

Patch said.

Lenny thought about this and relaxed his breathing a bit. He didn't want to freak Teddy out.

"I'm sorry Teddy. If you can do this and Patch can do this then I can do this."

Lenny said but braced himself.

Under his gentle urging the Ciera advanced towards the gates of the valley of the gigantic monsters. The sky was gunmetal grey and punctuated by narrow streaks of sunlight. The rotors that seemed to brush that canopy spun madly. It was a coordinated living and breathing ballet of madness and terror.

Lenny kept his eyes dead straight on the road ahead of him and tried to block out everything in the periphery. But like powerful magnets the great beasts pulled his eyeballs left and right. His mind raced and his muscles twitched and he started sweating.

Then from deep inside him it swelled a primitive survival mechanism had kicked in and the words one at a time came up through his throat barely passing through his brain

"Well... I've ... been... happy... lately..."

Lenny managed through clenched teeth.

"thinkin 'bout the good things to come..." Patch followed up.

"And I believe it could be..."

Lenny choked out a little bolder.

"Somethin good is so fun…"

Patch continued.

"That's not the right words!"

Lenny said.

Patched laughed hysterically and sang

"Cmon now – evah one get your ass on the peace train!"

Lenny joined in

"Ooooh ahhhh eeeeeh ahhhh ooooh ahhhhh – cmon, cmon, cmon!!!!!"

Winding through the morass of the giant monsters with their enormous spinning blades and whining, the Ciera and her passengers sailed. Sunlight fought hard to push away the grey eventually breaking through almost completely.

"Oh, Lordie, Lordie this peace train is movin into the light – to GOD be the glory!"

Patch said.

"Don't ruin the moment Patch."

Lenny shot back.

Patch laughed hard and sat up and bumped his busted foot against the rear seat. He shrugged it off and pushed his head between the seats.

"Oh Lenny, we doin it my friend! You and me and little Teddy over there! We doin it Lenny! We beatin them damn windmills!"

Patch rejoiced.

"Peace train holy rollers – ride on the Peace Train!"

Lenny shouted.

Together as the Ciera pushed toward the end of the valley, with the bright sun guiding them out of the jungle of steel trees and into the light Lenny and Patch sang together

"Oooooh ahhhhh eeeeeeh ahhhhh ooooooh ahhhhh… cmon, cmon, cmon!"

And when the last of the great beasts disappeared in the Ciera's rearview mirror Lenny and Patch hooped and hollered and high-fived each other, and Teddy.

It was like they won an actual war. You know, like World War I.

Lenny felt invincible. He secretly hoped the Aliens were watching. His new life was his. He was going to call her later that day. Patch was going to see his grandbaby. They'd made it past the toughest obstacle. Everything was going to be ok.

What could possibly go wrong now?

CHAPTER 27

Peace Train made Lenny think about his mother Monica Franks who had actually changed her name to *Sapphire Moonshadow* after she divorced Lenny Franks, Sr.

"I don't want my old name and I don't want his anymore."

Sapphire Moonshadow would say when asked about why she did that. At the time Lenny wondered if his mother was going crazy but the older he got the more sense it made to him.

Lenny always thought he was more like Lenny, Sr., but more and more felt maybe her genes and early guidance were sneaking in there a bit. *Sapphire Moonshadow* loved music and the arts and always took Lenny to concerts and plays when he was young.

She did say crazy things a lot over the years though. Here are some of the crazy things she said:

"There are new dimensions opening up all the time..."

"Mother Earth is in severe pain..."

"Things are opening up now for healing..."

"We can never know why the circus comes back…"

"Don't walk on the Indian burial mounds…"

Lenny opened up to her one day about the *Aliens* and she said

"Well… I don't know about that Lenny but do you know about the *Tristanians*?"

According to Sapphire Moonshadow the *Tristanians* were a race of beings from a different galaxy who brought the concept of peace to mankind.

"What do you suppose happened to them?"

Lenny asked her after she told him the story.

"Oh, they're long gone from this dimension. Since it didn't work here they've tried it on other worlds with varying levels of success."

After he called Lenny Franks Sr. and told him about leaving his big job and life he called *Sapphire Moonshadow*. Her reaction was predictable.

"Well there's a lot happening out there and we're all moving into new dimensions and planes so make sure you bring plenty of sage and an amethyst crystal with you for your journey. And try not to leave on a full moon."

Lenny didn't check the lunar calendar or anything, and was somewhat relieved the first night when he noticed a crescent moon. He did not own sage or an amethyst crystal nor did he purchase them for the journey.

Later after the Ciera burned down the thought that perhaps he might have done well to heed his mother's advice crossed his mind.

Chapter 28

The night after they conquered the windmills, Lenny found a good rest stop with a really nice bathroom. The odd pair settled into the Ciera and ate sandwiches they bought at the big gas station. When they had finished their dinner, Lenny poked around in the backpack and fetched the cellphone. He hadn't looked at it in a couple of days. She wanted her space and he had to give it to her. If he wanted to be with her he needed to respect what she needed. What he needed though was to hear from her and know that she thought about him and she said she would do that for him. He turned the phone on and saw a long line of messages. Here are the messages:

"How did you sleep my love?"

"I miss you Lenny"

"I burned my tongue on a bratwurst"

"I think the separation is doing us good"

"I'm out of gallon size plastic bags"

"Where are you exactly?"

"I just made cookies"

"The dogs ate all my cookies"

So, they were back to normal it appeared. She liked sharing all her little details about her day with him and he liked hearing about all of it. Whenever they spent time together everything was usually wonderful. But when they were apart, which was most of the time, then they had problems. She was young and needed to be young. He was old and had already been young. He had to let her be young. She had to remember he was old. He wanted to hear her voice, so he told Patch he had to make a phone call. Lenny got out of the Ciera and walked to a picnic table and sat under the stars and called her.

"Hi Lenny…"

"Hi Honey…"

And they were into it. They talked and talked and talked about their lives and what was going on. Lenny told her about Patch and the carwash and the Windmills. She told him about her world and her dogs and her roommates and how she just bought herself new clothes. They laughed and the conversation was easy.

When He said

"I love you"

She said

"I love you too Lenny."

And he would say it every few minutes. He liked saying it and he liked hearing her say it back. Then he started to talk to her about when he would see her again.

"I'll be in California soon maybe you could come see me."

Lenny said.

"Oh goodness me Lenny I think the separation is good for us. And I have so terribly much to do here."

Lenny Franks was at a point in his life where he really didn't know what he was gonna do and where he was gonna do it and he didn't care. He wanted to be happy. And he wanted her to be part of that. He thought she wanted it too, and she said she wanted it too, but there he was with Patch and Teddy in the Ciera and there she was a million miles away with her life. He was thinking more clearly about it now and really had made progress he thought. He wasn't looking at his phone every five minutes. He couldn't will it to happen. He couldn't make it happen. He wasn't going to work hard to MAKE it happen. He had convinced himself that that didn't work. He had seen it before with other things in his life. The harder he pushed, the worse it got. When he was just going along doing his thing, the phone would ring, something would happen. He knew if it was going to work he had to step back and ALLOW it to work itself out.

They finished the phone call on a very positive note and they said I LOVE YOU to each other more times. And then he said goodbye and turned off the phone. She was still in his life, but she wasn't here now. She was still his girl he thought even though he wasn't sure what that meant. He didn't know about everything happening for a reason but he had an unusual feeling of calm about the whole thing. Was he calm because she was still around even though she wasn't there or was he really calm because he was doing things different? Like getting a tattoo and showering at a car wash and making a new friend he wasn't trying to save and facing the windmills?

At that moment, he couldn't say for sure, but it didn't matter. At that moment, he realized that he couldn't do much about any of it no matter how hard he wanted to. He reasoned that at that moment the only way to be happy at all was that he really didn't need to know what was gonna happen next. The tide had already brought him some wonderful things if he just stopped and took a look at it so that's what he did.

Chapter 29

Lenny and Patch got up the next morning, did their morning business, and Lenny pulled the Ciera back onto the highway for the stretch drive to Venice Beach. There was a lot on Lenny's mind and he knew Patch had been around and had proven to be a good friend and listener so he said

"Patch can I talk to ya about some stuff?"

"Anything you wanna talk about Lenny I got nuthin else on my calendar today."

Patch said.

Lenny rubbed his head and looked out the window.

"It's just - it's kind of hard to talk about the war is all and maybe you don't want to hear about everything anyway."

Lenny said.

"Whatever you gotta say – you say Lenny." Patch said.

Lenny was right it isn't something everybody wants to hear about. In fact, you might not wanna hear about all of it either so just skip ahead if you want but this is kind of an important part of the story if you can hang in there.

"First off I got a couple big things to talk about. The first is my girl but maybe we can talk about that after the other one which is about what's been spinning around in my head since I was young."

Lenny began.

"I didn't really drink or use drugs till I was in College."

Patch sat quietly and listened intently to what Lenny wanted to tell him, even though his hearing was shot and he missed every third or fourth word.

"I guess I was at a party one time and I got drunk and somebody had some weed you know and so I smoked some. Like any guy would. Only I didn't stop with a few pulls. I smoked like 8 joints that night and found a guy to sell me some more. I'm like that I guess. Or I was like that where when I like something I do as much as I can."

Lenny took a deep breath and continued.

"So, I go to Los Angeles when I'm 22. I love it there. I love the ocean and I love the Palm Trees. I go to work for a guy in the TV station business named Ridgmont. It wasn't exactly the job I wanted but he was good to me and I was young and having fun. One night he had some cocaine and we did it at my little garage apartment in the Hollywood Hills."

Patch nodded and tried to keep eye contact with Lenny through the rearview mirror. Lenny was rubbing his head some more.

"Patch – It was awful. I kept doing more and more cocaine and the more I did the more I wanted to do and the less stuff I had. I sold everything I had so I could buy more. There were crazy nights and crazy times and I almost died. And then there were these things that I saw every so often in the Mirror when I was snorting the cocaine. I never told too many people this part before. I told Ridgmont one night when we were getting ripped together, but he just gave me this weird look and never mentioned it again."

Patch nodded.

"In the mirror, a few times I see these tall skinny purple alien guys all over the place and they're looking at these small phones except they don't look like any phones I ever saw and they're looking at their TV screens and on the screens, is like video from earth where people are just staring into these little phones all the time and not paying attention to anything else."

"Then I see like bombs going off on the screens and these tall Alien guys standing in a bunch of yellow cubes and it was really weird."

Patch nodded his head.

"I didn't see this stuff every time but a few times and I just got the feeling that these little phones were gonna kill us all. Then after a few times it stopped and I never saw the Aliens again. But Patch – when I got into my late twenty's and started seeing all these cell phones around for real and they looked like the ones I saw in the mirror and how people just keep staring into them well I get reminded of that and I think what if I'm right and I had this dream or whatever and cellphones are gonna end the human race?"

Lenny wiped the sweat from his forehead and looked straight ahead.

"My uncle named *UNK* drove to Los Angeles and found me and helped get me back to my home state. I screwed my life up worse there until one day when my other uncle named *Uncle Jimmy* got me to a hospital and I stopped doing cocaine and drinking. But I still think about those Alien guys."

Patch nodded.

"The hardest part was how everybody thought I was crazy and a failure after that. Man, even I wondered if I was crazy. Who knows, I probably am, and I probably was. I couldn't believe how bad it was and how far I had to go. But I kept after it Patch. I kept after it. I started piling up little wins and then a few more and then I got to be Lenny Franks and I had a good career. But after years of doing that – I just didn't want to be Lenny Franks anymore. And then well I met her not too long ago and thought maybe I could be a different Lenny Franks but with the world maybe ending because of all the cellphones and her being a million miles away well I just don't know exactly what to do. And then when she broke up with me before we got back together again I decided I had to get moving and do something for me."

Patch nodded and reached out and patted Lenny's shoulder and said

"Lenny that sure is some story. It's awful brave of you. You did a lot of stuff Lenny Franks and you ain't no failure. You just like the rest of us. You a human being Lenny Franks no more and no less and that means you gonna have stuff to deal with. And I'm proud of you for dealin with it. See, the God I believe in loves us because we make mistakes. We human, right? We gonna mess things up. We gonna do some good things too. But God, he don't care about none of that. He knows life's hard and he knows we almost never get it right. He don't keep a ledger or nothin. See, that's why I say all things all things happen for a reason. The reason Lenny is so that we don't have to go through em alone. I believe we ain't humans looking for God, but souls havin a human life. And God, he's there for all of it and he loves us when we in pain and when we happy and we full and when we hungry. And sometimes we get exactly what we need like when you and me met up. And lotsa times we get our asses handed to us, but either way, God's there with us for this whole crazy experience whether you ask him to be there or not. He don't care about football games or wars or math tests, but he there. All the time. And he was there with you when you was doin all that back then, and he here with you and me now.

Patch smiled.

"But what about the Aliens and the cellphones?"

Lenny said.

"Well Lenny I surely don't know about that. I will tell ya I never liked those cellphones. People in cars almost runnin themselves and me over every day and not talkin to each other. People so worried about everything except what they should be worried about. Lenny it's a beautiful world out there and nobody seems to wanna look at it or enjoy it or the little time they have with each other. You ask me I tell ya we'd all be better off without em. I know I don't have one. And the Aliens well who knows Lenny. Who knows. Makes about as much sense to me as anything else I've ever heard. But Lenny you and me we got each other and we got Teddy and you got your girl and what more could we want? And worryin about all of it ain't gonna do us any good or get us where we need to be is it?"

Lenny considered everything Patch said to him and he felt better. He felt better because he had unburdened himself. He felt better because he had found a real friend who wasn't asking him for anything and who didn't wanna be saved. He had a real friend who understood him and let him be however he needed to be and be as happy as he could right there and right then. Patch listened to him and he could feel that Patch wanted to help him. And he couldn't remember the last time somebody wanted to help him and didn't need or want anything in return.

Chapter 29

BL-002 slowed its engines and modified its course for final

approach for the rendezvous with *BL-001*. Thousands of giggling

Banglordians on each ship lined up at various windows and view screens

to watch the docking maneuvers.

They were happy but they were always happy and happy was a

choice and they preferred to make that choice as opposed to any

alternative. They learned generations earlier that some days plastic and

rubber are in large supply, and some days they aren't. Somedays they

might have a pain in their torsos, and other days they'd be fit as fiddles.

Plenty of days there would be salty rain to replenish their large saltwater

bins, and other days there would not, but that how they felt about any of

that was up to each of them.   Today though

they were unusually giddy at the prospect of having everyone back

together and so close to their new home.

SAL1111 was busy putting the finishing touches on his latest series

of encrypted messages to be integrated into the human tiny screen

networks to keep them moving right where they were all headed in the first place. The *Banglordians* had no remorse about expediting what was already a foregone conclusion. They had been around a while and if you've been around a while well – as the old *Banglordian* expression went – you didn't need a weatherman to know which way the wind blows.

RUFUS622 was in charge of executing the docking and he did this with precision. He had practiced for days on the simulator. The ships came together smoothly and the quiet but satisfying WOOOSH of the docking ports locking was meet by more laughter and cheers and tiny shit cubes all over the place on both ships.

BL-001 and *BL-002* were now one ship and contained the entire *Banglordian* race. *622* opened the latch on his side and *PAULIE213* opened the latch on his and they both laughed and shat tiny cubes.

213 crossed over to *622's* side and that made the whole thing official. And unlike humans there was no stampeding lineup or chaotic jockeying for the moving from ship to ship. Later there would be meetings to go over the final route to their new home and discuss who would be sent down with the scouting parties to give everything a good look and begin to coordinate the transition procedures.

1111 laughed and shat after his latest string of messages were incorporated on their new home planet. He had them at once scrambling

184

toward the big finale and getting excited to lineup for the newest version of the technology they already had and at a price that even *SAL1000110* couldn't believe they actually were willing to pay.

These humans really were one of a kind.

Chapter 30

Traffic in Los Angeles was just as Lenny had remembered it, and he remembered now why he fought so hard to forget about it. That was one of the screwy things about Los Angeles. The Ciera was stopped on the highway, and then it started again, and then it stopped and then it started. This went on for a long time and Lenny got frustrated. Patch lay in the backseat and looked out the window at all the buildings and big signs for movies and music and TV and shook his head and said

"Dang Lenny – People actually live in this place and drive in this stuff every dang day. Why would anyone wanna do that?"

"I know Patch – now that I'm here – I can't remember why I ever thought I wanted to come back here and live. But Venice Beach is different. And we can see the ocean and see what the tide brings in."

Lenny said.

"I'm lookin forward to seein the ocean. I never seen it before."

Patch said.

"Never?"

Asked Lenny.

"Nope."

Said Patch.

"Oh Patch, you won't believe it – it's like the biggest most wonderful thing there is to see."

Lenny said.

Patch sat up in his seat and said

"Lenny – tell me about this girl of yours."

Patch said.

Lenny shifted about, and smiled about the fact that this was the day he was gonna dump all his stuff, and began

"Well Patch I used to be married and I didn't wanna be married anymore and thought I wanted to be alone because it's easier. I dated a few women but nothing took you know. And then I was sitting in this meeting room for days and days and kept looking at this pretty girl who was sitting in front of me all the time. I swear Patch I just kept staring at her neck. It was so pretty. I even memorized it so I could think about it all the time. Then one day I told her I thought she had a pretty neck and

187

she smiled and right there I knew I was in trouble. But the good kind of trouble. See Patch, she's a lot younger than we are. A lot younger. We thought it was just fun but we ended up falling in love. Only she would get scared or I would get scared or one of us or the other would do the math on how old I was and she was and we'd flip out. We bounced back and forth a bit but kept coming back together. In fact, the reason I'm in the Ciera and heading out west is because she told me she didn't wanna fight for it anymore. That hurt. Really bad. I told her if she needed to go then that was that and that she should go and know that I understand even though I didn't. I mean I did but I didn't. You know?"

Patch nodded his head and said

"Oh, believe me Lenny I know. Ain't no man alive who don't know."

This made Lenny relax a little. He went on

"So, I was busted up you know. Really busted up. And then I started thinking about how I'm a handful for anybody especially somebody like that and then I started thinking about maybe because I didn't know who Lenny Franks was after the job ended and all maybe I was asking too much of her. Right before I met you she called and we've been talking and we both miss each other and we've both been saying all the right things. It's just that – I want to be with her Patch and she wants to be with me but I don't know if it's possible with the age difference and she having her world and me all lost in mine."

Patch considered all of this and said

"Lenny – It ain't none of my business you know but if you want I'll tell you what I think."

"Actually Patch, I'd love to hear what you have to say."

Lenny said.

"Well Lenny – here's the thing. Ain't no man can tell another man how he needs to be with his life with a woman. Women is tricky business. Lordie they all tricky business. We try and use the same way we are at work or with other men with women and that just ain't how it is. The heart sure is a funny thing and it want what it want and that's a fact. And Lenny we all got these pictures in our head about how it's supposed to be and how it's all supposed to look and that just screws everything up. Things can look anyway we want em to look. But Lenny you know me and how I think. Everything happens the way it's suppose to happen and right now you suppose to be in this car with me and Teddy. You suppose to figure out who Lenny Franks is and what Lenny Franks wants to do and who Lenny Franks wants to be. And if she the one then she the one and that'll all work itself out without you making it work out.

I know it's hard cause you miss her. Well, let me tell you somethin Lenny Franks she miss you too that's a fact. And she be there when you figure out what you gotta figure out. And if it's suppose to be it'll be. And lemme tell you this. You think too hard Lenny. I used to do that too but not as bad as you. What I do now is I pick out something like a rock or a tree or the sky and when my thoughts come racin in I go back to whatever I picked out. Thoughts will come in but we don't gotta turn em round and round. So just don't think so hard for a minute and when a thought comes in just go back to a rock or a tree or the sky."

Lenny listened carefully to every word Patch said as he nudged the Ciera through the downtown LA traffic and toward the Highway to Venice Beach. The road was opening up and the sky was clearing. And so was Lenny's head.

"You know somethin Patch? You're pretty smart for a homeless guy."

Lenny said. Patch let out a huge laugh and said

"And Lenny – you ok for a man who ain't got no clue about where he headed."

They both laughed for several minutes. Then Patch told Lenny the story about his life and his time with Jenny. After he finished Lenny said

"I know you think everything happens for a reason and all and that God is with you Patch but do you ever wish you had done something more or fought harder to stay with her?"

Patch shook his head and fought back a tear and said

"Every damn day Lenny. Every damn day."

And the two of them didn't speak another word until they pulled up into a parking lot a few blocks away from the Venice Beach Boardwalk.

Chapter 31

It was decided by the *Banglordian High Counsel* that scout teams be deployed to their new home world in groups of two. They needed boots on the ground and they needed to get further intel on this new world and on the layout for the gathering of the remaining humans after the bombs went off.

622 suggested that since they were hardly inconspicuous they would have to pick a place and a spot where they could blend in as best they could. They settled on what seemed like a perfect first test city – Los Angeles. More specifically Hollywood. From the monitoring on the screens and their previous intel they correctly deduced that America was the place most likely to have the highest number of humans locked into their tiny screens and not paying attention to anybody or anything else. With further monitoring they discovered that, in Los Angeles and in Hollywood in particular, that humans had these movie events for space movies where people dressed up like aliens. The *Banglordians* laughed in chorus when looking at images of what humans thought aliens looked like but figured they would fit in just fine around places like that.

It was decided that *Herb888* and *Carl656* would be the first pair to go to Hollywood to do the scouting. They would take one of the small capsules that had sophisticated anti- radar devices to avoid detection and land it in a nearby open space and turn on the shielding mechanism to keep the craft hidden and then proceed on foot to Hollywood and take a look around. They did need to wear some sort of pants not in an attempt to blend in but for collection of the tiny yellow shit cubes which they figured correctly would be dispatched with great frequency and force, so they manufactured some very odd-looking trousers.

The journey took only two earth days, and they found a spot near the observatory and set the craft down and exited it and looked around. *888* was hungry from the voyage and *656* decided he could eat too, and they couldn't believe the ready supply of plastic bottles just laying around. They sucked several bottles each and began walking and noticing all the tires on the cars, and they started laughing and communicated to each other that there was seemingly an unending food supply on their new home. Both noted this in their preliminary reports. They walked down streets they had already mapped out and they had been schooled on navigating the primitive traffic lights prior to being deployed.

Some humans honked horns when they saw them and some waved. Most humans didn't notice them and not one thought anything was unusual about two eleven-foot-tall, ten-inch-wide furry purple aliens sucking up plastic bottles and jiggling their odd trousers while meandering down Hollywood Boulevard. It was like they were invisible.

Chapter 32

Lenny and Patch walked from the parking Lot toward the Venice
Beach Boardwalk and Patch had picked up a plastic bag and was
collecting plastic bottles and whatever else he thought may come in
handy. Lenny understood that this was how Patch lived and so every now
and then he picked up a bottle too. Patch dug through a trash can and
picked up a small can of paint and some glue and said

"You never know Lenny – You never know."

Lenny shrugged this off. The two made quite a pair but nobody gave
them a second look. Patch as a homeless man knew about feeling
invisible all the time, and lately, Lenny was starting to feel invisible too.
They moved through an alley and when they came out the end there was
the Boardwalk and on the other side – so big and beautiful and churning
was the Pacific Ocean. When Patch saw the incomparable vision in front
of him he dropped his bag and fell to his knees. The whole thing was
really quite emotional if you wanna know the truth about it.

"Oh Lenny, you were right! This is the most beautiful sight I maybe
ever saw."

Patch said.

"Didn't I tell ya?"

Lenny said.

He liked when he could do things like this for other humans. When he could be there and show em things that he got a bang out of. He decided that even the new Lenny Franks liked that and that he was gonna stay with that part even in his new life.

They spent the day wandering around up and down the boardwalk and picking up this and that and putting it in Patch's bag. They even took their shoes off and waded into the ocean and Patch cried some more. Lenny liked it when Patch got so emotional he cried. All day long Patch said things like:

"Oh Lenny, ain't this the best world we got?"

"Lenny what did I tell ya about how beautiful this world is?"

"Lenny I'm having a great day."

And Lenny couldn't argue with any of it. On that day, he didn't think about what his life would look like or what he was gonna be or do or even what was gonna happen with him and his girl. He just enjoyed the day for what it was. He and Patch talked and he bought Patch a hamburger at one of those little places with rickety chairs and dirty tables outside and they took turns walking and sitting. Late in the afternoon Lenny said

"Patch let's bring the bag back to the car and see if we can find a better parking spot where we can watch the sun go down and sleep in the Ciera."

Patch said

"Oh Lenny, I don't know if I can take watchin what's gotta be such a beautiful sunset."

Lenny smiled and told Patch he was sure he could handle it. They walked back to the car and Patch put the bag with the bottles and the glue and the paint and all the other crazy things Patch had picked up and then drove the car to a parking lot near the beach. It cost 20 dollars but Lenny felt like splurging. This was a great day, and it was gonna be fun to watch the sunset with Patch, and sleep near where you can actually hear the tide come in. Lenny parked the car with the trunk facing the beach as the sun was starting to disappear over Malibu. Patch asked him to open the trunk. Lenny grabbed the backpack from the front seat with Teddy in it, because he wanted Teddy to be there too. He popped the trunk and Patch dug through the plastic bag, and pulled out a crushed pack of cigarettes and an old plastic lighter he found earlier in the day.

"You care for a smoke Lenny?"

Patch asked.

Lenny used to smoke but he hadn't had one in a long time. He thought about and thought about living in the grey and said

"Sure Patch – what the hell."

Lenny said.

Patch did the honors, lighting Lenny's cigarette first and then his own and they sat on the bumper of the Ciera and watched as the big orange ball dropped out of sight. Lenny loved the moment and liked the cigarette and enjoyed smoking it. He took the last puff of and dropped it to the ground and crushed it under his shoe and grabbed Teddy and the Backpack and said

"Cmon Patch – Let's go see what the tide brings in."

Lenny started away toward the beach with the old bounce back in his step and Patch stood up and smiled and thought this really was the best world we got and what a good new friend he had in Lenny.

Then Patch flicked his still burning cigarette into the air and followed Lenny toward the beach.

For better and for worse, and the good news and the bad, was that both of them were lost in that perfect moment, and both of them were completely unconcerned and blissfully unware about what was about to happen next.

Chapter 33

So now it's time to meet another important character and her name is Kathleen. Here's a little back story on what her deal is because she's about to help Lenny and Patch out bigtime after the Ciera was incinerated.

Kathleen was about the same age as Lenny and Patch and grew up in the southern California area, and currently lived in a house in Venice Beach a couple of blocks from the scene of the fire. She had two teenage boys named Kyle and Kevin and she raised them by herself. Her husband left them shortly after Kevin, who was the younger one, had been born. He had not been heard from since, and Kathleen wasted not one minute thinking about him. She was independent and capable, and had a decent job and money in the bank. The boys were well looked after.

One of Kathleen's hobbies was carpentry, and she was in the middle of renovating her garage into a place that she could rent to vacationers. One of the upshots of companies in all industries finding new ways to gouge their customers while simultaneously dropping the level of service

200

to new lows, was that there was this whole series of humans popping up and giving each other rides and a place to stay and even a car to drive for much more reasonable prices. Kathleen saw the opportunity and wanted in on the action. She was very handy and that came in – well – handy. She had framed the inside of the garage and with a friend's help she ran the electrical and put in a couple of windows and had the sheetrock cut and the tile already laid on the floors. The toilet was in and the shower tile was sitting in boxes. It was slow work and she was anxious to get it done, but something always distracted her. Life always seemed to get in the way. She didn't have a boyfriend for a variety of reasons, with the most important being, she had more than enough shit on her plate.

Every morning she'd sit in her back yard and have coffee and do the crossword and the word puzzles and go to work and then come home and take care of the boys. She made time every day to work a little on the garage, and then cook dinner and then pay bills, and then clean out this closet or that, or her office or fix something, and then she'd take a nightly walk down toward the beach at sunset to clear her head. Then she'd go home and collapse out of sheer exhaustion and start the whole thing over the next day. The world sure could take pieces out of a woman.

Today had been a tougher day than normal. She had saved up her money to buy new windows for her house. This was one of those jobs somebody else had to do. Ordering them was a nightmare of course and it took the sales guy and the measuring guy three trips to get it all figured out. After waiting for 4 months, which was 2 months longer than promised, the workers arrived 2 hours late that morning and they arrived with entirely the wrong windows. She didn't notice this until she returned home from work and they had all been installed. Just for good measure the installers chipped plaster all over her house and hung a new door backwards and upside down. It was always something. The dinner she made for the boys went largely uneaten because Kevin was at a school function she had forgotten about and Kyle had soccer practice that she had marked for the wrong day. She ate a quick bite and poured herself some wine in a plastic cup and began her walk to the beach. Hopefully the walk and the sunset and the wine would settle her down.

As she walked, she chewed and chewed on the damned window company and on not only what a pain in the ass it had already been, but on what would be the walk through hell itself it was going to be to get it done right. She knew, like everyone else knew, that she had to summon the strength of 10,000 humans to walk through that gauntlet of sending emails, and making phone calls, and sitting on hold, and getting shifted from one person to the next, and unreturned calls, and customer service surveys, and on and on and on. She knew that the strategy from the company's side would be the same as always. Companies routinely now employed the strategy of giving the customer an unlimited number of hoops to jump through and that if they were willing to do it – to do all of it – perhaps the company would eventually fix the problem and offer a small refund for her trouble.

Perhaps... but the numbers said most customers would tire and just give up.

As the boardwalk and the ocean started coming into view she exhaled and took the last big gulp out of her cup and clenched her other fist and screamed inside of herself. She looked toward the heavens and asked god or whoever was up there

WHY WHY WHY IS EVERYTHING SO FUCKING HARD ALL THE TIME?!!!

She took a deep breath, and gathered herself, and looked toward the sun which had just disappeared over the mountains and she wrapped her arms around herself and put her head down. She was lost in the quiet for just an instant. And then she heard it.

BOOM! PUK-OOOSH! WHOKSH! FITSHSHSHSHSH...

Kathleen turned her head left toward the sound of the explosion and saw what looked like a car bursting into flames. She saw people dashing here and there and she stood motionless for a few moments and watched the spectacle. Kathleen was not the type of person to take out her cellphone and video the episode. In fact, she was the kind of person who rarely had her cellphone on her. She didn't have it with her now. She walked toward the melee.

As she approached the parking lot and moved closer to the scene of the incident she was almost run over by a guy wearing a shit-stained blue T-shirt on roller skates playing a banjo. She inched up closer and joined the circle of largely homeless humans standing several feet away from the foul-smelling smoldering late model Oldsmobile Cutlass Ciera. She turned to the guy with the banjo and said

"Whose car is that?"

And the guy pointed at a pair of guys about her age who were a black man and a white man and said

"I think it belongs to them."

The white guy was rubbing his head and holding a backpack and a Teddy Bear and the black guy looked like he was speaking some kind of consoling words to him. She approached them. Kathleen was not the type of person to be afraid of talking to other humans. She arrived to their side as the last flames were being extinguished and looked at the white man who appeared to be crying and who had a little vomit on his lip.

"Is that yours?"

She asked him.

"It was a few minutes ago."

Lenny said.

"Well – coulda done without that huh?"

Kathleen said.

Lenny looked up at her and smiled because he remembered that line from another one of his favorite movies, *Tommy Boy* and said

"Ya think?"

And that made all 3 of them chuckle a bit.

"Do you guys live around here?"

Kathleen asked.

"Oh no ma'am we actually was livin right there in that good old Ciera there that just burned down. That there is Lenny Franks and Teddy and I'm Patch. We just come a long way and Lenny here is trying to find hisself and I'm gonna see my grandbaby. But we sure don't know what we gonna do now."

Patch said.

"You got no place to stay then?"

Kathleen asked.

"Ummm nope. Well we had one but it looks like the tow truck is headed this way so..."

Lenny said.

Kathleen put her hands on her hips and thought about it for a minute. Then she asked

"I take it you 2 being new in town and all and living in that mobile palace over there you don't have jobs or anything either?"

"You take that exactly right."

Said Lenny who was actually starting to like this smartass Kathleen person.

"You got any money?"

She asked Lenny.

"A little. We can find a motel or somethin for tonight I suppose and then figure it out."

Lenny said.

Kathleen considered this and then said

"Look why don't you two come to my place. I got a garage in the back I'm turning into a little place for people to rent and if you want I'll give you some sleeping bags and I got some food and you can decide in the morning what you wanna do. My kids think I'm nuts anyway so what the hell. Sound good?"

Lenny shook his head as he took the ticket from the policeman, who came up to him as the wreckage was being hosed down and the tow truck was pulling in. He didn't have a lot of other options, and he actually thought this Kathleen person was ok, and in fact just happened to be in the right place at the right time. As he accepted her generous offer and they all started walking away together the thought entered his mind.

Do some things actually happen for a reason?

Chapter 35

"Unbelievable STOP Entire planet busting with Plastic and rubber all over the place STOP Humans paying us almost no attention STOP Except for occasional image capture with us using tiny hand held screens STOP Humans also not paying attention to each other and just looking into tiny screens especially at string of drink shops STOP Plastic cups at drink shops especially robust and fortifying for our diet STOP Heading down toward one of the huge salt water repositories STOP Intel appears to confirm we can blend in on Venice Beach Boardwalk and check out repository STOP lower garments working to collect cubes well except we keep having to dump them out STOP Hilarious all the way around down here STOP Next report in .000012 Microfledgers STOP"

Herb888 & Carl656 preliminary notes report for attached detailed report to *Banglordian High Counsel. Earth date – October 3, 2017.*

Chapter 36

BANG BANG BANG BANG BANG BANG BANG!

Lenny sprung out of his sleeping bag and scoured the garage in the pre-dawn light for the source of the percussive noises that jarred him awake from an almost perfect slumber.

"And good mornin to you Lenny Franks"

Patch said with hammer in hand while leaning against a board of sheetrock he had just finished pounding into one of the walls.

"What the hell are ya doin Patch?"

Lenny asked.

"Well Lenny I thought I'd get an early start."

Patch said.

"On what?"

"On Miss Kathleen's walls here."

Patch said as he bent over to grab the next board.

"Wait wait wait wait…"

Lenny said as he struggled to his feet. As he moved toward Patch, the garage door burst open and Kathleen stomped in in her bathrobe and bare feet and her hair was covering some of her face.

"What the hell are you two doing in here?"

Kathleen asked.

"I was wondering the same thing."

Lenny said.

They both looked at Patch.

"Well Miss Kathleen I know a thing or 2 about buildin things and with you being so nice to us I thought maybe me and Lenny could help you out here."

Patch said.

Lenny looked at the floor.

"Patch it's not even sunrise yet."

Kathleen said as she stepped closer to the wall to examine his handy work. She rubbed her hands along the edges and squatted down to check the fit.

"Hmmm."

She said and then got to her feet.

"Not bad Patch. Is Lenny as good with his hands as you are?"

Kathleen asked.

"Not at this…"

Lenny said smiling. He couldn't help it. Somebody was gonna hang a slider, he was gonna knock it over the wall. She smiled back and then looked around the garage.

"OK I'll tell ya what. If you guys wanna finish the sheetrock we'll see how that goes and talk about what's next. Then you can stay here and trade the roof over your head for the work."

"Oh, Miss Kathleen that about the nicest…"

Lenny cut Patch off.

"Sounds good to us but what's for breakfast?"

Lenny said.

He was a good salesman after all and so he was attempting to negotiate a better deal.

"Eggs. And I think I got some bacon in there. Come in in about 15 minutes. And Patch hold off on the work till at least 8 will ya? I got neighbors. And kids."

Kathleen said.

"Yes Ma'am"

Patch said smiling.

After she walked out the garage door Lenny rubbed his head and turned to Patch and said

"Well Patch we might not have the Ciera and I might not be able to figure out who I am and you might not get to see your grandbaby for a little while but it looks like we got jobs and a place to stay and food to eat."

And Patch said

"I told ya Lenny. If you just pay attention this is the best world we got ain't it.?"

Chapter 37

Twelve other scout teams had been deployed and the *Banglordian High Counsel* gathered in the large conference room on *BL-002* and drank saltwater and laughed and shat as they read the reports. It really was unbelievable.

Not too long ago their own existence was in doubt. Not too long ago they had no idea where they would relocate. Seriously, what planet would provide the exact kind of food and shelter they required? What planet in the universe would possibly have natural salt water repositories all over the place? What planet would be empty and available? Sure, this planet was inhabited but who knew the tech insertion would go this well with this particular group? Certainly, their hard work paid off but even they had to acknowledge the unbelievable stroke of luck they had in running into these idiots at the exact right time.

Once this was a race that had some promise. Each earth century was bloodier than the last for sure, but young races were prone to doing things like that before they started to turn it around. But not humans. Humans showed an uncommon flair for always making the wrong choice with technology. Instead of feeding each other they spent their money on building bigger machines to rip the place apart. Instead of using technology to nourish their minds they adapted technology to make their minds mush. Instead of dealing with each other fairly they chose to knock the ever living shit out of each other. They worked each other to death. They made laws not for each other but for a tiny few who wanted to have it all. They worried and fretted about all the wrong things. They ignored their own clusters and viewed other clusters as dangerous when really it was all just one big cluster. Unlike *Banglordians* and other advanced races, humans thought different color shading, or what book they read, or where they lived made them all different or threatening. They took almost no time to appreciate what they had. They didn't laugh much. They chose to be pissed off. And they were headed not toward enlightenment or even incremental progress but total destruction.

The Banglordians just gave em a little nudge a little before they were ready for it.

And now in just a few days the whole thing would come together. The new piece of technology to replace the old piece of technology would come out and humans would line up in front of the gathering and shipping stations. And at the same time – if *SAL1111's* calculations were correct – the greatest agent on their behalf – the human in charge of the most powerful human cluster on earth would start launching the biggest weapons they had and that would be that.

Banglordians didn't believe in God, but if they did, they would have been singing his praises at the top of their lungs.

Chapter 38

For 3 solid days Lenny and Patch worked in the garage. First, they put up all the sheetrock. Then Patch showed Lenny how to put plaster over the nail holes and the cracks and get it ready for painting. It was good and honest work, and it kept Lenny's mind occupied and off all the other stuff that he usually chewed on. If fact, when other thoughts did pop into his head, as they always did, he practiced looking at the hammer and tried not thinking. And damn, but it actually worked. He was spending less time chewing on all his thoughts. He was enjoying what he was doing. He thought that maybe this carpentry business wasn't so bad after all. He thought that he might be able to get his brain around a different kind of life. A simpler life. A life where you did an honest job, and got to sleep someplace nice, and eat good food around people who were actually reasonably good to be with. A life where he didn't always have to think about things so hard. But he did think about her. He felt good about her and they would share messages every now and then and they would talk on the phone. It seemed to be going well even though he was a million miles away and so was she. On the last phone call though she said something that stuck in his head

"Who knows Lenny – but I think we'll see each other really soon."

Did that mean she was coming to see him, or that she thought he was going to come back and see her? He felt at peace with it though. He felt like he was in a good spot with her and that worrying about it never did anybody any good anyway. He knew that of course but only now as he stopped thinking so hard all the time was it actually seeping in a little.

It was the middle of the afternoon, and Patch and Lenny had just finished taking the shower tiles out of the box to look at them when Kathleen appeared inside the garage.

"Hey guys – looks good!"

She said.

"Thanks. I got Patch up to speed finally and so it's coming together."

Lenny said. Then

"What are you doing home so early?"

Lenny said.

"Oh, I got fired from my job today."

Kathleen said.

"What?"

Lenny asked.

But she waved it off dismissively.

"It's OK – I hated that damned job anyway and now I got time to work with you two on the garage!"

Kathleen said.

She seemed genuinely happy about the development Lenny thought and so he said

"OK Great. Patch can use the help anyway."

Patch laughed.

"Oh, Lenny Franks you a funny man."

Patch said.

"Guys let's celebrate. I'll take you both to dinner down by the beach. C'mon we'll make it an early dinner. The boys are out doing whatever it is boys of that age do so it'll be just the three of us."

Kathleen said.

Lenny and Patch finished putting their things away, and used the cleaning wipes on their hands and faces and got as tidy as was possible, given that they were still wearing the same clothes for three days. Kathleen didn't seem to mind Lenny thought, and he was right about that. Kathleen liked Lenny and Patch. She liked having new humans around and especially new humans she hit it off with. She thought Patch was sweet and actually was flirting with him a bit, and she thought that Lenny was well – Lenny.

The three of them were laughing and talking as they made the walk toward the Venice Beach Boardwalk, and Kathleen said she had a nice little place she always liked to go. They found another one of those places with rickety chairs and dirty tables outside and sat down and looked at the ocean and watched the humans go by.

"Ain't this the most perfect day and ain't this about the most beautiful world there is?"

Patch said after they ordered.

"You know what Patch – it ain't all bad."

Lenny said and they all lifted their water glasses for a toast. Lenny said

"To the best world we got!"

219

And they all clinked glasses.

"You know what Lenny I think you actually findin yourself pretty good."

Patch said. And then

"I mean I don't know how the old Lenny Franks woulda handled the Ciera burnin down and losin all his stuff and all but this here Lenny Franks seem to be crusin along pretty good."

"You know what Patch? I can't tell ya I even know why I'm ok with all of this but I am. Maybe it's now that you got me not thinking so hard all the time and taking deep breaths and lookin at the hammer every so often. You are right though. The old Lenny Franks woulda lost his shit over all this but somehow, I ain't that worried about it. I've been thinkin here over the past few days about how I've always managed. Somehow. Someway. And being with you both and you saying how all things happen for a reason and how the world is such a beautiful place well I don't know. I'm not saying I believe it all but... I mean look at Kathleen here and you. I got two friends I never had and frankly I prefer both of y'all's company to most of the people I used to hang around with anyway. And my girl well she'll be with me or she won't. I mean I hope she will I really do and I'm not gonna lie but I can't do anything about that. I'm ok being just how I am now. I'm not noticing how dumb everything is or how crazy everybody in their cars are or how much they charge a guy for a coffee or anything. I mean, I notice it but then I just think about something else. I laugh more. I'm ok watching the people and looking at the ocean and working in the garage. I could use some new clothes though Patch and you could too and maybe tomorrow we could..."

And Lenny stopped in mid-sentence. Standing right across the boardwalk and looking at him was her. His girl. She came to find him and there she was. And when their eyes met he had the feeling that everything was gonna be ok. Although he conceded in his own head that sometimes he wasn't always right about all of that.

Chapter 39

Herb888 and *Carl656* loped along the Venice Beach Boardwalk and waved at humans and the dumb old humans waved back. They had picked up the waving business in Hollywood. And every now and then, humans stopped to do image captures with them with their tiny screens. These humans must have thought they were from the movies or something but still… *Oh well*, they thought, and they just kept on with their leisurely stroll shitting into their trousers and laughing.

They had some very large saltwater collection bins on their home planet, but they had never seen anything like the size and the scope of the Pacific Ocean repository up close. They did get a few odd looks from humans when they bent over to suck the water right up from the shore line but that came with the territory. They decided that they had seen enough of the Boardwalk, and that they'd head back toward the one of the large collection and shipping facilities to prepare for the festivities which would be coming in two earth days.

They looked this way and that, and watched humans staring at their tiny screens and they shat some more. They stopped on the boardwalk and took one last look at the enormous salt water basin, and made some notes for their next report.

As they were about to walk away from the Boardwalk however, they were approached by a very small cluster of four humans. Two males and two females. Three of them just stood there looking and laughing at them and the fourth walked up right up and looked them up and down. He touched their purple fur and looked around at all the humans looking at their cell phones. And then he spoke to them softly at first and then louder and louder

"It's you, isn't it? You guys are real aren't you! I knew it! I fucking knew it! It's here isn't it? We're done aren't we? And it's all because of..."

And he pulled his cellphone from his pocket and continued

"THESE FUCKING THINGS!!!"

888 and *656* were puzzled at first but then remembered their intel about the glitch in the subprogram software of the *SNS1022* chip and thought maybe they ran into one of the humans who had a little sneak peek. They shared the *Banglordian* version of a nod which was to thrust their pelvises at each other.

Lenny turned to Patch and Kathleen and his girl and said

"Look at these two. These aren't costumes or actors or anything. These are ACTUAL ALIENS!"

223

Kathleen laughed and said

"Sure they are Lenny…"

But Patch remembering the story moved closer and regarded the giant furry creatures.

"Lenny, these really them?"

Patch asked.

"Yeah Patch I'm positive."

Lenny's girl looked at the Aliens and then looked at Lenny and said

"Oh, my goodness gracious me Lenny, what on earth are we going to do?"

And Lenny smiled because he like it when she talked like a 70-year-old woman.

Chapter 40

656 and *888* loped slowly away from Lenny and his three compatriots up the Boardwalk north toward Santa Monica. Lenny followed them for a bit, and the three followed Lenny, but Patch increased his pace after a few minutes and tracked Lenny down and said

"Lenny what you fixin to do?"

"I don't know but I gotta stay with em Patch."

Lenny said.

Patch grabbed Lenny by the left arm and stopped him in his tracks. Patch was a strong man.

"Lenny, we gotta think about this some. We got the girls with us and all and well if these are the Aliens and they're dangerous and all we best be careful for their sake and we need a plan."

Patch said.

Patch released his grip, and Lenny stopped and turned toward Kathleen and his girl and then spun back and watched the Aliens walking further away and said

"Patch this could be it though! What if this is it?! We gotta do something!"

Lenny could get really animated when he was excited and he was rocking back and forth and rubbing his head and yelling loudly. His girl walked up and rubbed his shoulder and neck and said

"Lenny this is terribly bad, isn't it?"

"I think maybe yeah it is."

Lenny said.

Kathleen joined the other three and although she wasn't quite sure of what was actually going on, she deferred to the others.

Patch said

"Lenny, it seems to me we need to talk serious about this and come up with a plan. I mean nobody seems to be bothered by these big purple fellas so maybe it ain't that big a thing you know?"

"Patch I listened to you a lot these past few weeks and I'm a better person because of it. But you gotta listen to me now. All of you gotta listen to me. We gotta come up with a plan because the way the world is nobody is payin attention to the stuff that really matters. Look around Patch! Nobody is even paying attention to two eleven-foot-tall purple aliens for Chrissake!!!!!! That's gotta tell ya something. And I don't know what I'm gonna do but…"

Just as Lenny was fumbling for the right words and looking around trying to formulate what their next move might be, the guy in the shit stained blue T-shirt with the banjo on roller skates glided up and stopped right next to Lenny and said

"Brother, Brother, Brother – it's them ain't it?"

And Lenny shook his head and looked him dead in the eyes and said

"Yeah. It's them alright."

"Brother, Brother, Brother, I've been waiting and preparing for this day for a long time and I know exactly what we gotta do."

Chapter 41

This particular week, in this particular administration, in the West Wing of the White House in Washington DC, was beyond anything Kelly Phelps had ever seen in his life. And Phelps rightly thought he'd seen it all. He'd been all over the world and had served his country with great honor and distinction. He was experienced, still sharp as a tac, and suffered no fools. And even though he wanted nothing to do with this torrential and chronic shit show in the center of the most powerful residence in the world, he felt duty-bound to accept the job as White House Chief of Staff when it was offered. He thought somebody with at least half a brain, and a smidgeon of common sense, and at least a vague understanding of how things in the United States Government work should join this unholy circus and try to put the clamps on this idiot before the whole fucking thing collapsed. But every day was like – as they used to say in the military – several monkeys trying to fuck several footballs at the same time.

On this warm early fall day, Phelps got to his office unusually early at about 4:30 am, to begin sifting through the previous day's wreckage, and work on past and what he knew would be present and very near future damage control.

"Fuck me."

He said as he started to plow through the enormous stack of folders.

"What in God's name is wrong with this fucking guy?"

In his heart of hearts, he didn't really blame his boss for being how he was. He was how he was. He was how he always had been, and he wasn't interested in being any other way. Most people were like that, Phelps thought. All bosses in this era had narcissistic, sadistic, and uncaring tendencies, but nobody he had ever seen or met or been around or worked for or with had em this bad. The country was fucked, and the people didn't know what the fuck was going on or what the fuck to do about it so they put the erratic and borderline psychopathic sonofabitch in the chair.

This was on them...

"Christ..."

He muttered to himself as he moved on to the next pile of briefings and news clips. As he drank his coffee and rubbed his temples and tossed one folder after the next from pile to pile he wondered why he hadn't just gotten that sailboat and fucked right off for good. He was close, he almost pulled the trigger, and then he got the call and got sucked back in. And every day the shit was worse and worse. Floods and storms and fires and wars followed by impotent and chaotic responses. Press conferences that were handled like dogshit. Nobody on message – not that there really was one and that was another problem. Drone strikes and troop movements and more bodies. Mass shootings and violent protests. People tearing each other apart. No diplomatic tact with the rest of the world. Mistake after fucking mistake and some of it criminal, but that wasn't Phelps's problem. Not yet anyway. He had seen the files, and had ample cause to believe that the day before the findings would be revealed and the charges would be levied, the thin- skinned bastard would press the button and push the world to the brink. But there were always brush fires to put out, and hectic challenges every five minutes. No new legislation that was worth a shit, and his boss couldn't keep his fucking mouth shut or his fingers off his cellphone. And the First Family and the members of The President's revolving door inner circle were all – each of them – grossly unsuited and wildly unprepared for any of it. He figured correctly, and it was always confirmed when he spoke to his counterparts around the globe, that he wasn't the only one wondering what horrific calamity would befall the land of the free and home of the brave.

As he kept scanning through the tragedies and the missteps and incompetency's there was a quick KNOCK, KNOCK on his door and his assistant, Anthea Jean slipped in with another cup of coffee for him, offered him a meek good morning, and asked him if he had seen the social media binder yet.

Governance used to be a tough business and now it was fucking impossible, and a lot of it had to do with this new social media feeding frenzy. His boss was leading the charge by waking up every day with a hard on, and sniping at this thing or at that person and then everybody else had to deal with the requisite and predictable daily fallout that ensued. The news media ate it up because it was good for business, and the good citizens of the greatest country in the world had nothing better to do than follow the shitstorm and weigh in with their own inane drivel, firmly rooted in the perpetually swirling unbridled fear and unprecedented malignant ignorance.

"No. Not yet… Why? What's he done now?" Phelps said with his head down.

Anthea was a good assistant who kept her head down, did what she was told, stayed out of the way and never offered much of an opinion on anything. She never told those even closest to her anything that went on in there. That made her an uncommon employee and sought-after commodity who would always find work. There really were only a handful of people like that in the world when it got right down to it.

"Well he's not up yet but there are some interesting – ummmm – *sightings* around the globe."

She said *sightings* like she was saying it for the first time and not sure how to pronounce it or what it actually meant.

Phelps scratched the back of his neck and forced his head up from the pile on his desk and leaned back in his chair and said

"What *sightings* exactly?"

Phelps mimicked her pronunciation of the word.

"Well it seems that there are pictures and videos going around from all over the world on the internet and on TV showing these very tall purple creatures posing for pictures and drinking ocean water and eating plastic bottles and dumping little yellow cubes out of their – ummmm – pants or whatever it is they're wearing and well it's just the strangest...."

He cut her off and waved the photos to which she was referring toward his hands. She handed them over to her rapidly aging much older boss, and with a creased brow, he flipped through them, regarding each one quickly and then he summarily plopped the whole pile into the trash under his desk.

"Look – He's got a lot going on today. The Senate is voting – or not voting on the infrastructure bill, and that douchebag Roan and his buddy old father time *McDickwad* have bugs up their asses over the healthcare thing, and he's got a hockey team coming in for photos, and he's gotta meet with the Joint Chiefs to see if they can keep his twitchy trigger finger off the button for at least one more day - - - and he hasn't *twitted* anything yet and - - - Anthea Jean – I don't have time for this shit. But – Thanks for stopping by."

She smiled and left silently and Phelps took the coffee she set on his desk and shook his head.

Of all the fucking things to bring me…

he thought.

Kelly Phelps sighed deeply and went back to his pile, but he was quickly ripped away a few seconds later when his cellphone chimed in with the familiar and ominous siren song. This President of the United States woke up as he always did – not with his eye on the job, but on some crazy sideshow bullshit and he did what he does every day – he fired large bore cannon shots out into the world from his little phone. Now - he had just tweeted something derogatory about some famous athletes and another ball bust about sagging Sports TV ratings and the day was about to get very, very long.

The former General hung up the phone and opened his computer and went to the website he used to visit to daydream a bit but in that instant, he decided – TODAY was the day that he was going to buy that fucking

sailboat.

CHAPTER 42

So, here's how *Banjo* got to be *Banjo*.

Kevin Davis spent his formative years on the East Coast, and had a relatively normal middle-class upbringing. His parents were of modest means and they left their only child to fend for himself. That's how it was in those days. Nobody packed his lunch, or drove him to soccer practice, or put a helmet on him when he rode his bike, or went on weekend campouts with him. Parents had their own shit to worry about and the kids would be fine. And actually, for the most part, kids were more than just fine.

He could best be described – as those around him used to describe him – *dumb in school but smart on the bus.*

He never cared much for reading or writing or algebra or biology or any of the usual things the world continued to regard as extremely important to drill into small children's heads every day. Kids wouldn't be taught to balance their checkbooks, or figure out mortgage interest, or automobile insurance, but they had to memorize the periodic table of the elements.

Kevin was an accomplished smartass and the prototypical *Class Clown* and this got him noticed for all the right and wrong reasons. The same behavior that landed him regularly in the Principal's office, also got him laid every now and then. Women like funny and he was a laugh fucking riot.

Kevin found out early how to get attention and how to matter. He was a gifted conversationalist, and had a flair for storytelling, and for composing and delivering his own razor-sharp one liners. One of his favorites was his response whenever someone would prompt him to recite the story about when he shit his pants. He'd quickly pop back

"Which time?"

He was also born understanding a very important and basic tenet that too few honor students ever grasped.

If he bought something for a dollar and could sell it for two – he could make money.

In High School, he sold a little weed and ran poker games and made book for anyone who wanted to throw a bet down on a football game. As he continued through his educational experience, his circle of friends and acquaintances expanded and so did his business. He'd barely graduate –

but when he did – he did with a six-figure bank account. Not bad for a kid with no real formal education in the 1970s.

Kevin spent two weeks the summer after his senior year in Los Angeles and was immediately hooked on the weather and the ocean and on the good times and the cool vibes. After spinning his wheels for three more years in New Jersey honing his skills as an industrial soup salesman's salesman, and swelling his bank account, he decided California is where he needed to be.

He'd say

"I just get tired of my balls shrinking into 2 tiny frozen peas in my sac every time I get into my car in the winter..."

The week after his 21st birthday he put everything he cared about into his 1979 Cadillac El Dorado and made the cross-country trek. He had never been to Las Vegas, but because of his fondness for playing cards and betting games, it was certainly going to be a stop along the way.

Kevin liked to have a good time and he could hold his stuff. He got louder, and usually funnier as the night went on, and he would throw money around for more booze and food, and at strippers, as he wore down customers and closed a lot of deals he couldn't remember he closed the following day. Even at 21, he was drinking a lot and smoking a ton of weed. He had plenty of money, and was clever and sharp but he was starting to spring more than a few leaks.

That stop in Vegas on the way to LA was the beginning of the end. He figured he'd spend a night or two, and horse around and have some fun. He wound up limping out of town six weeks later with almost all of his bankroll gone and his prized car sitting in a pawn shop parking lot.

He hitchhiked to LA, and got a motel room near Venice Beach. He cleaned himself up and made two or three more runs up the hill, until he finally crashed and burned for good. In the spring of 1984, during a long bender of booze and weed and cocaine he snapped. He told the few friends he had left that while he was snorting cocaine off the mirror he saw – clear as a bell – visions of eleven-foot-tall, furry purple Aliens passing out these weird square phones and taking over the world.

He shared that with his parents over the phone, and they promptly flew out and found him, and used some of the little money they had to check him into a psychiatric clinic for a week.

After seven days of intense therapy and a series of experimental drugs, 26-year-old Kevin Davis told his counselor that he wasn't crazy, the rest of the world was. He cautioned the counselor to stay away from technology, and offered to him that, if his calculations were right, the whole planet had about 30 years left.

Kevin's parents returned to New Jersey and never spoke to their son again. He walked out of the Clinic understanding what his mission in life was to be. He was going to prepare and be ready for when the time would come. He found a pair of Roller Skates in a dumpster, and won a banjo that he still could not play in a dice game on the Venice Boardwalk in 1994. He kept it strapped over his shoulder. Kevin Davis shed his given name and told everyone to just call him, *Banjo*.

Banjo was a bit of a local attraction as he was seen by tourists and passerby alike day after day. He spent years and years on the Venice Boardwalk building a network with other homeless people. Some of whom saw what he had seen, and more who had nothing else better to do. They met regularly and they formulated plans for when the day would come.

Chapter 43

Here's another example of how tough the world could be on the average human. And this one is gonna be a little painful when it's all said and done.

Joshua Williams had no desire for fame or fortune, and that was for the best given that neither seemed to care enough to grant him even a cursory nod.

He arrived on the west coast at age 5, after his Mother and Stepfather hauled him out there. He saw how dangerous dreams were. He watched his Stepfather struggle with an unending series of acting audition rejections, and he observed his mother work 80 hours a week just to keep a roof over their heads. He remembered her expression – was it relief exactly? – when his Stepfather left for an audition one day and never come back. He was 10 years old. His mother did a fine job of getting him through school, and his milk-chocolate-colored-skin and gruff good looks helped him gain modest acceptance from everyone, but he fit in with almost no one.

At 14 he was a pretty good baseball player.

At 15 he shredded his knee and that was that.

At 16 he got arrested for being in the wrong place at the wrong time.

At 17 he dropped out of school because he and his mother needed the money. He got a job at a local fast food place and met a pretty girl who had the best smile he ever saw.

At 18 he thought he'd marry her. Then one night when she was out with friends for a birthday celebration their car was hit by a drunk driver, and all three girls in the car were killed.

At 19 he found good work at a T-shirt making shop. Later that year the place burned to the ground and the owner left town.

His mother died the following year.

Before she died, she told him about his real father and gave him his last-known address. He was curious and alone, and located a friend of a friend who had seen him, and they made arrangements to speak on the telephone. It was a short call – his father Eugene seemed embarrassed and Joshua was a man of few words.

His Father said

"Son I know I ain't perfect but I know we'll see each other again because this is a beautiful world and it's the best world we got so I believe it and you gotta believe it too."

He told him that one day he'd find him in Los Angeles. Joshua never heard from him after that call.

And on like that it seemed to go for several years.

At 27 he caught a light gust of wind and got a job at a family owned company that made tortillas. There he met a serious but kind woman named Angelina and the next year they were wed.

Theirs was a marriage between two extremely prematurely disillusioned and inconsolably sad people who wanted to try and salvage something from their respective wretched earthly experiences. Angelina's story was as sad as his, but they made a life together. Misery and company and so on.

He and Angelina became valued employees of *The Squishy Face Tortilla Food Company* and were both promoted and the two-combined earned a living just above the poverty line. They rented a small house in Torrance, California and spent every free minute and every extra piece of change painting it, and fixing it up, and making it a home. Despite their relative proximity to the Pacific Ocean, they almost never made it to the beach. Theirs wasn't that kind of life.

The next year Elijah was born. Angelina stayed home and made telemarketing calls during the day, and Joshua joined the nouveau desperate herd and picked up a few extra dollars ferrying people around greater Los Angeles in his own car. That was its own special kind of indentured servitude, complete with foul smells, and footprints all over his backseats, and rudely behaved people.

There was never enough time and hardly ever a spare dollar at month's end. The company they worked for had been surviving but had to make some tough calls. That's how it was for everybody but especially the little guys. They wanted to keep their entire workforce employed but the price was steep. Management swapped below average health insurance for horseshit health insurance. They reduced wages by 5 percent across the board. Everybody including Joshua swallowed hard but swallow they did, every nasty last drop of it.

What else could they do?

One day Joshua caught a small break when he won a drawing at work where they gave away a new digital tablet computer thing. It was a few days before Elijah's 7th birthday.

Joshua was so excited when he brought the voucher home and showed it to Angelina. Together they made plans to surprise their young son with a trip to the big computer electronics store with no pillars, for the unveiling of his new birthday gift.

Joshua was feeling wonderful the rest of that week.

Life was so hard. The excruciating days that all ran into each other – the toiling for toiling's sake – the brutal nights of driving dullards and drunks – there was the perpetual credit card debt – the high prices on everything – the shitty expensive but cheap food – there was never a vacation – but there was bad health insurance and overpriced car insurance and high gas prices and expensive utilities and taxes and fees and more fees - the only reason he had the Cable TV they couldn't afford was so Elijah could watch while Angelina made her phone calls.

Joshua couldn't fathom how much it was going to cost to adequately provide for his son – hopefully college someday – to buy him sporting gear and pay for team fees and trophies and traveling – he didn't want to even think about other activities and money he'd half to shell out for his only child just to stay within shouting distance of everyone else. But he would do it. He would do it or die trying. He would show Angelina and Elijah and himself that he was different. Different than the father he never knew who never came to see him or the Stepfather who left and never came back.

Yeah it was hard. Fucking right it was hard. But Elijah would get the chance he never got. Joshua would figure it out. He'd go take classes and get an even better job to earn more money for Angelina and Elijah. He was no stranger to hard work and there was supposed to be this deal in the greatest country in the world – if you work hard – if you keep your nose clean – if you take care of your family – you'll reap the promises. You'll have a big SUV and a sports car in the driveway and 2 chickens in your pot and money to spend and a nest egg to retire on. You'll own a nice home with a big yard and you'll go to ballgames and you'll go on great vacations and you'll buy your wife pretty things and you'll eat out at nice places and you'll be successful. It's all up to you is what everybody said. You can do anything is what the people on TV told everybody.

Except he'd been working 80 – 100 hours a week every week since he was a teenager and every single day he wondered when any of it might show up.

Well this week a little tiny piece of it did. He finally got one, and he really needed one and it was a big one. This week it would be HIS first grader who would get a flashy new toy. This week it would be HIS

245

family walking into one of those fancy phone stores and leaving with something shiny and new. This week it was HIS wife and HIS son who would look at him like a success.

They'd take Elijah out to his favorite place for hamburgers after the big surprise, and they'd go home and eat the strawberry angel food cake Angelina could make so well, and they'd laugh and be just like a regular successful American family. He might even take a little money out of his emergency fund and get Angelina something pretty. They'd put Elijah to bed later and maybe – he thought – maybe – he and Angelina could spend the rest of the night like an actual husband and wife. He wouldn't drive that night. Fuck it. He was going to have one perfect day with his family and give his son a memory his father Eugene – or – what was it his father wanted to be called?

Oh yeah – *Patch* – *Patch* – *what the fuck kind of a name was that?*

Well he was going to give his family a memory that that sonofabitch had never given him.

Chapter 44

They all assembled around the makeshift village on the grass and under the palms adjacent to the Venice Beach Boardwalk. There were piecemeal tents, and cardboard box dwellings, and broken shopping carts, and plastic tarps, and plastic bags filled with plastic bottles and beer cans, and dusty blankets, and piles of dirty clothes, and tin bowls with food from garbage cans, and torn sleeping bags, and odd and useful and useless random items laying all over the place. The dingy cluster of humans and ratty objects emitted a foul odor, and that combined with the general distasteful appearance to the carefree tourist or busy local dweller, kept outsiders away.

The people in the messy village were also dusty and dirty and raggedly scattered about. They survived on their own wits and the small kindnesses of others. The former being the most useful, and the latter increasingly these days in shorter supply. There were about 80 homeless people gathered around the circle. Some paid closer attention than others to the program. Some were incapable of paying attention at all. But they were all there. They had come to homelessness in Venice Beach from different parts of the country. The stories of how they became homeless in the first place were all so much the same. Most had no families or safety nets. Most had some degree of mental illness. Most had had jobs of one kind or another at some point. Some were military veterans, some were mothers and fathers. All were daughters and sons. None of them saw this as their future when they were little children.

Charlie came from Chicago and grew up wanting to be a fireman.

Paulie was from Minneapolis and thought he would be a drummer in a rock band.

Maureen had been a lieutenant in the army but always thought she was going to be a schoolteacher.

Brooklyn had been a schoolteacher but her husband and two children died in a fire.

Schlitz drove an ambulance but couldn't put the bottle away.

Jace and Sparky came from different places and were the oddest pair and had grown to become the best of friends. Jace was six-foot, seven-inches tall, and always wanted to be in the circus. Sparky was exactly a foot shorter, and wanted to be a preacher. Watching the two of them walking around together was a sight.

Billy GEE would say

"Hey Jace – when Sparky gets tired do you just pick him up like a monkey and carry him around on your shoulder?"

Billy GEE used to be a Professional athlete, but he blew all his money buying several large houses and was wiped out during the crash of 2008.

Danny was a drug dealer and he snorted up all his profits and eventually was beaten within six inches of his life. He couldn't hear anymore.

Iris had been a hooker until she got too old and nobody wanted to pay her for sex any more.

Baggy and Irene and Portia and several others had seen images of tall purple Aliens in the early 80's while snorting cocaine and they either snapped or snapped to it or both.

Lenny and Patch and Kathleen and Lenny's girl were standing near the front and next to Banjo, who was about to give his speech in front of the large semi-circle of the sitting and lounging and standing hoard. Lenny and Patch fit in nicely. Kathleen and Lenny's girl looked like a pair of glistening platinum candelabras at a garbage dump.

"You've all seen em now. They're here."

Banjo began his address solemnly.

He continued

"But my brothers and my sisters we've been planning for this and preparing for this and so we're ready and it's up to us. I know it won't be easy but we can do this. We know what needs to be done."

"AMEN … COCKSSSSSUCKER … VRIPP… SONOFABITCH… Help us all help them all brother Banjo FUCK FUCK FUCK"

Lanky had turrets but he was on board.

"You're damned right brother Lanky…"

Banjo continued

"A lot of us knew about these godawful cellphones and about the Purple Creatures for a long time. The rest of you heard the prophecies from all of us and we need you too. We're going to proceed with the plan. We're going to scour the boardwalk and ask people to throw their cellphones away and if necessary we're going to rip them out of their hands!"

There was a small swelling of clapping and cheering. Constance pulled down her pants and took a leak over a cardboard box but she yelled and screamed in assent.

"The away groups will go to the technology stores in the neighborhood and work the lines. We will not be deterred. We will succeed!"

Banjo proclaimed with a flourish to an even more enthusiastic round of cheers and applause. "And now…"

Banjo continued

"I'd like to turn the meeting over to our new brother Lenny!"

After they had met on the Boardwalk and watched the two tall Purple Aliens walk away, Banjo shared the common story and the plan with Lenny and Patch and Kathleen and Lenny's girl. Banjo was amazing, Lenny thought, as he simultaneously got Lenny up to speed and through a series of hand signals and short commands organized the gathering in just a few minutes. The two men spoke the same language, and the chemistry was instant and evident. Since Lenny was closest to the current calamitous world, Banjo suggested that he speak to the group, and share a scouting report on some of the obstacles they may encounter with this new breed of overly distracted and grossly apathetic humans. His girl said to him after Banjo suggested this

"Oh Lenny, I love you and you're about the smartest man in the world and you're so good at selling people on things I think it would be just a terribly wonderful idea if you got up there and said a few words."

Lenny gave her a hug and a kiss and they both smiled and stared at each other. She could always be so supportive and inspiring he thought.

Lenny took three steps toward Banjo, and bowed his head and then lifted it back up and scanned the quieted throng. He looked at Kathleen and Patch who were holding hands. He looked at his girl and she smiled the way she always smiled at him with her teeth clenched and her head slightly cocked. This gave him confidence. He winked at her and began

"I was here in Los Angeles a long time ago. I was just a kid and I made a lot of mistakes. I coulda been here on the Boardwalk with y'all and maybe that woulda been ok except that Lenny Sr. had money and so I got to figure it out without living outside. But like Banjo and a lot of you I saw em. I saw the purple Aliens. I saw the square cellphones and I saw the world blowing up. I thought about it from time to time but I couldn't make sense of it. But it still bothered me…"

Lenny started rocking back and forth while rubbing his head and he went on

"It bothered me every time I saw people staring down at those damn things especially when they were driving a car. It bothered me over the years seeing how people kept paying more and more attention to the dumbest things. It's gotten so much worse lately. Most people don't know who's in government but can tell you who's on what reality TV show and what video of cats is the best one this week. Most people are tired. Most people don't have any money. Most people are sad. Most people are fat. Most people don't look at flowers or babies or the ocean and think how wonderful those things are. Most people watch news all the time to see who got blown up or burned up or to watch the police chasing cars on TV. They can go three-deep on an offensive line depth chart and they don't know what the bill of rights is. Most people are scared. Most people are stuck and have no idea how to be unstuck."

"UNSTUCK... VRIPP... WHOOF WHOOF WHOOF... MOTHERFUCKER... STUCK... COCKSUCKERS ARE STUCK..."

Lanky belched out.

"Right... Stuck..."

Lenny said and kept going

"Anyway, it's way worse than ever. And they hold onto those cellphones like they're gold bars. It's gonna be really hard to get them to take their eyes off of em and look at anything else. They might get violent. They're gonna yell and scream like a toddler if you take his candy away. It won't be pretty. But I think if we stay at em and get em to look around and see the purple aliens and get em to see what a beautiful world this can be that maybe we have a chance. If we can get Venice Beach – we can get Santa Monica..."

Lenny's confidence grew and his voice started to rise.

"If we get Santa Monica – we can get Los Angeles..."

The crowd around him started bustling and throwing

"Yes!"

and

"You tell us Lenny"

and

"FUCK VRIPP FUCK!"

into the air with increasing fervor and determination.

"And if we get Los Angeles... IF WE GET LOS ANGELES... WE GET THE COUNTRY!!! AND IF WE GET THE COUNTRY – WE GET THE WORLD!!!!!!!"

They all yelled and cheered. They were all – each of them and all of them together – ready to follow Lenny and Banjo off the cliff's edge.

This scraggly crew, these forgotten and invisible refuges of society, these dusty and dirty and disposable and diseased men and women. This group of misfits now banded together and cheered with one voice. These humans, who until that moment almost always felt less than human because that's how they were treated by those around and above and even below, were now humanity's last best hope. And sadly, it wouldn't be enough.

But by God and by Christ they were gonna give it a good go.

Chapter 45

After the rally, they all agreed that they'd effort for a good night's sleep, and get busy first thing in the morning. Banjo stayed in the village and worked with Portia and Baggy on making out the assignments. Lenny and Patch and Kathleen and Lenny's girl went back to Kathleen's house to find Kathleen's boys and work out what they would do. Banjo suggested that he handle the Boardwalk operations and mobilize the troops, and that Lenny and Patch join Jace and Sparky early the next morning as the group's primary away team to work the lines at the cellphone stores in the neighborhood.

Patch went with Kathleen to go pick up her sons, and that left Lenny and his girl some alone time in the garage.

"I've missed you."

Lenny said.

"Well I've missed you too Lenny."

She said.

"I'm so happy to see you but I guess I kinda wanna hear what made you come all this way and back to me."

He said.

"Well I don't know but I didn't like spending my life without you. You're not easy to be with all the time Lenny. And I guess I'm not either. I needed to find that out I suppose. And even though it's only been a few hours I can tell you're different. You seem more relaxed. I mean even though the world is ending and all you look great and you sound like you're not so crazy like you were a few weeks ago."

She said.

"You know honey I think you're right. I know I'm not easy. I know I've been my own worst enemy. For the first time in my life I see that. Patch helped with that actually. The Ciera burning down helped with that…"

He said.

"Oh, my goodness gracious the Ciera burned down?"

She asked.

"Oh yeah – I didn't tell you about that. It's a long story but actually it's funny. If you hadn't left me I never would have driven out here. And if I didn't have to go pee so bad I never would have run into Patch. And if the Ciera hadn't burned down I wouldn't have met Kathleen and her boys and me and Patch wouldn't have found work or even met Banjo and the rest. I actually believe that all things kinda work out the way they're supposed to."

and he paused and then said

"Ain't this the best world in the world?"

And she smiled and hugged him and said

"Oh Lenny, I'm not the easiest person either and I never asked you how I could help but I want to. And yes, this is a marvelous world."

And then they kissed, and Lenny led her to the sleeping bags on the floor and they celebrated this best world there was and their reunion in the most glorious way possible.

Chapter 46

Lenny drifted back toward consciousness fully sated and blissfully content. He was floating on clouds as he felt her under his arm. He was twisted up in old sleeping bags on the cement floor of a garage. He hadn't had a real shower since the car wash. He gave no thought to any of that. Or to the fact that he had no car and no money and no job and the world was about to end. Through half-shut eyelids, he glanced at the hammer on the floor beside him. It felt good not to think so hard all the time. This moment was perfect and he was the happiest man in the world.

As he starting coming around he was helped back into the real world by the sound of the garage door handle rattling. Someone was trying to get in. He took his arm off her side and kissed her on her warm, sleepy cheek and started toward the noise. He was naked.

"Patch? Kathleen? That you?"

Lenny asked as he approached the door with his hand over his pecker. A naked man when threatened will cover his pecker first, and not his head or his heart and doesn't that sound exactly right and tell you all you need to know?

"Lenny, Lenny, Lenny – it's us! It's Sparky! And Jace is here with me!"

Lenny remembered he had given Banjo the address the night before.

"Oh. Ok. Gimme a sec."

Lenny said as he located his stinky clothes and put them on. He opened the door and slipped outside to join them so his girl could sleep some more. He was like that and not everybody was.

"Lenny this is gonna be a big day!"

Sparky said excitedly as he slapped Jace on the back with the palm of his hand several times in succession. Each time it made this weird popping sound. Lenny considered for a moment how this resulting sound was possible.

"It will be indeed."

"GOD YES!"

Jace said as he made this weird motion with his lips.

Lenny shrugged whatever that was off, rubbed his head a couple of times, and scanned the driveway and the back of the house as he wondered where Patch was. Or Kathleen. Or her boys.

"Hey you guys seen Patch?"

Lenny asked.

"The big black guy from last night?"

Jace said deadpanned and loud.

"Yeah – you seen him?"

Lenny asked again.

"How bout this guy Jace calling him a big black guy?"

Sparky said to Lenny as he rubbed his hands together and laughed. These two were a pair.

"Nah we haven't seen him. That's great. Now three of us will have to do the work of four and the weather sucks."

Jace said with severe resignation.

He was not the most optimistic soldier for the cause.

"It'll be ok big man – you can handle it."

Sparky said as he popped him on the back a few more times.

Lenny was mildly amused by the interplay of his two new compatriots but needed to figure out where everybody was. He sauntered across the driveway and went to the back door of the house. He turned the knob and went inside and peered into the living room and saw Patch and Kathleen rolled up in blankets on the floor. The end of the world prompted more than one late night liaison at that residence Lenny thought.

Good for Patch...

Patch's eyes were opened and he bellowed

"Oh, good morning Lenny and ain't it a beautiful morning?"

The volume and tenor of his announcement prompted Kathleen's eyes open, and she looked up at Lenny and said

"Hey Lenny. What's up?"

And then she turned and gave Patch a kiss on the lips.

"Same old stuff you know. My girl's sleeping on the floor in the garage I've been living in for a couple of days and my new best friend is laying naked in blankets with our new landlady and there's twelve feet of humans in the driveway doin some kind of Laurel and Hardy act and the world's about to end... How bout you guys?"

Lenny said.

Patch chuckled but snapped to it.

"OK Lenny what you want us to do?"

Patch asked.

"Well let's all get dressed and meet in the driveway in 15 minutes. That work?"

Lenny said.

But before either could answer Jace, who had snuck in from outside, boomed out from directly behind him

"Hey – anybody got anything to eat around here?"

"The big man loves to eat!"

Sparky said smiling as he bounced across the threshold while rubbing his palms together.

"Sure. I'll fix something after I get dressed. Why don't you guys go sit in the Kitchen. I'll just be a minute."

Kathleen said wrapping a sheet around herself and walking toward the staircase.

Lenny's girl wandered in and joined the group just as naked Patch was uncoiling himself from the blankets.

"Oh, my goodness me!"

She shrieked after regarding Patch's genitalia.

"Jesus Christ Patch, you got a permit for that thing?"

Jace said smirking and looking around the room.

"How bout this guy?"

Sparky said popping Jace on the back.

Lenny shook his head. Like or not, this was the special, chosen group that had the fate of humanity in their hands.

Chapter 47

Today was worse than the day before, and the day before that, and the day before that, and so on, but that was business as usual with this group Kelly Phelps decided as he walked the hall from the elevator to the White House Situation Room.

Phelps had just heard from his guy at Justice. The indictments were coming down within the week. If Phelps heard, he was pretty sure his boss had heard. And if what he had heard was accurate – it was even worse than what everybody thought was the worst- case scenario. His boss was in deep shit and was about to face the full force and unimaginable ire of the entire United States Justice Department.

It was probably the reason the most powerful man in the world took to social media an hour earlier and announced his intentions to give those "Cocksucking maggots on the other side of the world…" – and he actually used the word "Cocksucking" in his posting – "a lesson the likes of which the world has never seen…"

Phelps pocketed his cellphone, negotiated the hallway corner swiftly, and nodded at the young guard at the door. He marched in and took his usual place at the large conference table in the anteroom. He regarded the familiar faces and they regarded him. Each man's expression reflected the other's. Foreboding. Dread. Resignation.

No one said a word as they waited for the President to arrive.

A moment later the large man wrapped in a US NAVY satin jacket and tight fitting MTUSASA ball cap strolled in with his head locked down on his cellphone but barking orders to the aides in tow.

"And fuck the press conference! We're not doing any more Press Conferences! They'll get it from my speech. Mother Fuckers all of em. When we going? I want to do it in 10 minutes! Get it ready for fuck sake! The Oval Office! And bring me some chicken nuggets and a coke! Now!"

Phelps shook his head and put his hands in his lap. He had been working with a few other serious and pragmatic colleagues on an emergency bill to supersede exactly what they had all privately worried about. But they couldn't get the damned thing done quickly enough. He had a personal escape plan for himself and his family that was ready to go at a moment's notice, and he had made the call as he walked from his office to the Situation Room. The chopper was fueled and his wife and

266

children were already on the way. From the chopper to the airstrip, and to the jet which was standing by. From the jet to the island, to the rover, and then to the bunker. The whole thing would take just under six hours. If they had six hours…

"Alright it's time. You know no other President had the balls for this guy but I do, and now we're gonna show them all that you can't keep laughing at the United States of America."

The President said to stone silence. And he continued

"We're going to launch in – what is it Harvey – six minutes is the first strike?"

Harvey was the President's son-in-law and was standing right behind the seated President.

"Ummm – yes something like – yes six minutes."

"Christ…"

Phelps muttered to himself. The whole thing was just unbelievable. And this fucking kid to boot. He wondered if this was the first time he heard the little pissant actually speak.

"OK then I'll make the announcement from the Oval Office to the American People and that will be that. You guys keep me in the loop ok?"

The President said to no one in particular before jumping up and leaving the room.

"And where are my fucking Chicken Nuggets?!!!"

He belched on his way out the door.

The door closed and Phelps looked around the room. There was nothing anyone could do. The founding fathers had fucked em, and the supreme court had fucked em, and the voters really fucked em. The group had kicked around the 25th Amendment several times but couldn't get enough people on board and figure out how to get it done. They all had kept individual and group dialogues going with each other and justice but there was nothing they could do. The final attempt to enact emergency legislation stalled and so here they were. Five minutes from first launch.

"God help us."

Phelps said as he stood up and prepared to start the journey toward the chopper.

Chapter 48

The war was going about exactly how you might expect. On the Boardwalk, the homeless army was doing their best but no cellphone possessing good citizen gave a shit.

"Hey – get the fuck out of here!"

"Get a fucking job why don't ya!"

"Get your stinky hands away from me!"

Those and other similar refrains were belted out by some and echoed by others along the concrete strip for the better part of the morning.

And there were casualties.

Here are a few:

Baggy took an elbow to the jaw and lost eight teeth.

Billy Gee got in a fight with a middle-aged woman and was arrested.

Lanky got wrestled to the ground and peed on by a group of vacationing fraternity boys.

Portia and Iris got spat on.

The away teams had it worse. On the Boardwalk, the soldiers of the homeless Army would target one or two individuals, or a small group at a time and usually could get away. Working the line of dozens of people outside the cellphone stores meant facing an entire unit.

Lenny had his backpack with Teddy in it. He and Patch and Jace and Sparky were strafing the line at the cellphone store in Santa Monica. He made the decision to have Kathleen and the boys and his girl wait across the street. It was the right call. Kathleen had mentioned she might have an idea what she would do while they waged their battle. When Lenny asked her what she meant, she said

"You let me worry about that."

At the store's outside line, Lenny tried the reasonable salesman's tack.

Patch always opened with something akin to

"Ain't it a beautiful day in the best world we got?"

Jace had Sparky on his shoulder trying to reach over people's shoulders and pluck the tiny devices out of their hands.

None of these approaches worked even remotely.

People were locked into their cellphones scrolling through mindless drivel. They paid no attention to Lenny and his compatriots except to admonish or shoo away. Annoyed that they could not continue to focus solely on the inane without interruption, pockets of them banded together to repel the unsolicited and unwanted advances. It got ugly.

Patch approached an excited young family. A father and mother and their young son were waiting in line.

"Daddy – I'm really getting a present here?"

The boy asked.

"Well it's your birthday and we're here so... maybe... if you're a good boy..."

His father said with a smile.

"What is it Daddy What is it?"

The young boy asked.

"Well if I tell you it won't be a surprise will it Elijah."

His father said patting him on his head.

"Well if it's your birthday you should get something pretty special."

Patch said to him. Patch had overheard the conversation and had worked his way up next to them.

"Sir I don't mean to be rude but please move along."

Joshua said to Patch.

"Well I ain't tryin to upset anybody but there's something I need to tell ya about what's goin on here with the world."

Joshua stepped in front of his wife and son and regarded the old man.

"Sir the first time I was polite. This is the second time. The third time ends with my fist across your jaw." Joshua warned him.

"I'm sorry sir. I'll move along. You and your family have a good day now. Happy Birthday young man."

And Patch let this family be, and shuffled off toward Lenny.

+++

The world can be a cruel place and things don't always work out. Patch *was* right all those years ago. Patch and Joshua did see each other again. Patch even saw his daughter-in-law and grandson. But none of them knew it and none of them ever would.

Too many times in life, there aren't tidy packages with pretty bows. Too often, there's just holes that never get filled up. Too frequently, things just happen that defy logic or explanation.

Closure is what you sell yourself so you can live with disastrous mistakes and unavoidable horrific tragedy.

And happy endings are for the movies. This is just a book.

Chapter 49

"Global Intelligence gathering from all teams confirms more than adequate supply of plastic and rubber an saltwater STOP Conspicuous movement for away teams no issue due to apathetic human inhabitants STOP Leader of World's Largest cluster AKA OUR GUY DOWNSTAIRS preparing imminent nuclear launch STOP Advise away teams in potential blast areas to look for caves STOP Estimate BL-001 and BL-002 section separations and arrival in .00000008 Fledgers STOP After blasts will advise on landing zones STOP Recommend readying human gathering teams for collection and shipment STOP Would like to acknowledge SAL1111 on contributions to help distract and occupy and steer humans toward extinction STOP See you all at our new home soon STOP"

Rufus622 General dispatch to all Banglordians. Earth date, October 21st, 2017.

Chapter 50

"My fellow loyal Americans...

I speak to you from the most powerful office in the world which, as you can see, looks even more powerful and more beautiful than ever before because of the renovations I ordered and personally oversaw. You know, I own a lot of office buildings, some of the largest and most beautiful in the world but many, many, many people have told me that this office now looks like the most beautiful and powerful of all the offices I own. And I own a lot of them, believe me.

You elected me by the biggest popular voting margin in history because you know I'm the best Leader that you've ever had or will ever have. No President has ever accomplished what I've accomplished in such a short time. Harvey, how many bills have we passed? Many, many, many bills. Great bills. The best bills. All the bills that frankly no other President had the courage or the deal making abilities to pass. It's been unbelievable really.

I want to thank my sons and my daughter and you Harvey for your loyalty. Loyalty is important you know and if you're not loyal to me well then, I'm not your president. But for those of you who are loyal to me and it's a lot of you, so many, many, many of you, more than any other group in history, I have great news for you.

Before I was President the world laughed at the United States of America but nobody, and I mean nobody is laughing now. Believe me. Believe me.

Because America is the best country, the best country. Of all the countries that have ever existed, America is the best. And right now, America is the best it's ever been because I'm the best President you ever had. In fact, we're working right now on getting rid of the two-term limit on the Presidency. That's a great idea. I said when I got in here and Susan you'll remember this, I said hey, why is it that a President can only serve two terms? Nobody thought of that before. So, we're getting rid of that and you'll see how great that's going to be. Believe me. Believe me.

The other reason America is the best country is that God loves America more than he loves any other country. That's true. Many, many, many Priests and other Religious people have told me that. And I love God. I do. God's great. Truly, truly great. He's been great to me.

In fact, I know for a fact that God loves the job I'm doing here. I've read that in lots of places.

Today, we're doing something that's very exciting. Really exciting. I know you're going to be excited. You see, we can't let the rest of the world laugh at us. And "Missile-Man" has been laughing at us. And he's got Missiles! He does. And he keeps threatening us! I say to myself, What's the matter with "Missile-Man"? How come no other President has ever dealt with "Missile-Man"? Well, today we're going to deal with him the likes of which the world has never seen.

Right before I came in here to address all of you who are so loyal, so loyal to me, I gave the order and put in the codes and we've launched our missiles at "Missile-Man."

I told you. Exciting isn't it. This is going to be so great, so great.

And they'll be so beaten back and surprised by this that we expect – Harvey – we expect their surrender later today right? Right. See, very exciting.

And oh, listen, did you know that the deficit has never been lower? That the market has never ever, ever been higher? That unemployment is the lowest it's ever been? You wouldn't know that if you watch the unreal news but all that's true. It's really true. It's sad that I don't get all the credit I deserve. Very sad.

We've done so well, so well, it's really incredible. I promised to make the *United States of America Soar Again* and today is just another example of high we're soaring.

I'll speak to you later today about the surrender, and I'll have more news on the two-term limits thing, won't we Harvey, won't we have that today? Ok. Well you'll find out soon I can promise you that.

So, thank you my loyal supporters, you know who you are. You're the real Americans, the ones who were here first and who aren't going anywhere, believe me.

And may God continue to bless Me and The United States of America.

Chapter 51

They gave it a good go. Lenny Franks and his army of homeless people. They were the first to see what was going on and everybody had to give them that. Except that humans being how they were nobody gave them that.

Banjo and his Boardwalk Brigade gave it all they had but nobody cared. The away teams threw themselves into the battle with great might, eagerness and fury, but nobody cared. Lenny's army was battered and beaten not so much by fists, but by apathy. Humans were all so busy rushing from this thing to that and looking at their cellphones and craving distraction from their miserable lives the whole time that they couldn't spare a minute to save themselves.

It was a turkey shoot.

The first blasts from what was once the most powerful country in the world hit on the other side of the ocean, and people took a few seconds to look away from their cat videos and food pictures to watch the bright flashing lights on their tiny screens. But only a few seconds. It wasn't in their backyard so they didn't really care so much. And anyways, there was this video of a guy with duct tape over his mouth and juggling carrots on this popular TV show, so they all had to watch.

But the counter attack came to their backyard in just minutes and some of them actually looked up just in time to see it.

New York was the first city in the United States to get it. Then Washington DC. The White House was incinerated just as the President finally got his chicken nuggets and was looking at social media. And then Chicago fell. Then more hits to the western half of North America.

More Missiles were aimed at Europe and Russia and the rest of the world and from all sides and the sky was ablaze with a crisscross of missile exhaust. By days end, almost 4 billion people were dead. By the end of the week another 3 ½ billion more perished.

Cellphone technicians worked round the clock that week and kept some of the service going, but none of them were promised or paid overtime.

The *Banglordians* separated their ships and sent them off to myriad destinations across the globe. It didn't take long for them to spray the remaining humans with the sleeping powder and stack them in the cellphone stores for temporary storage, and then load them onto the ship sections and dispatch what was left of humanity to the stars.

There were a few stragglers who averted the blast and the wind by hiding in underground shelters who survived including a group of 8 in Los Angeles. 9 if you counted the Teddy Bear.

Four men. One black and three white. One very tall and one very short. Two women. Both white. One older and one younger. And two teenage boys. And one old Teddy Bear.

When the bombing started, the four left the line of humans waiting for the newest technology, met the gals and the boys, and got in the older woman's car and drove to her friend's house in the Hollywood Hills. He had a large and spacious and well stocked underground bunker. The woman used to sleep with him and she knew he enjoyed her many talents. And when men enjoyed that you could get just about anything you wanted. she had a hunch about this guy after listening to Lenny and Patch over the past couple of days.

His name was John Ridgmont, and he was a very successful computer graphics producer, who when partying one night in 1984 with his young protégé, saw a series of hallucinations involving tall purple Aliens, small cellphones, and the end of the world.

THE END

www.senselessproductions.com

www.ingramcontent.com/pod-product-compliance
Lightning Source LLC
Chambersburg PA
CBHW032209190626
46810CB00019B/2363